ARIZONA ARGONAUTS

ARIZONA ARGONAUTS

BY

H. BEDFORD-JONES

GARDEN CITY   NEW YORK

DOUBLEDAY, PAGE & COMPANY

1922

PRINTED IN THE UNITED STATES
AT
THE COUNTRY LIFE PRESS, GARDEN CITY, N. Y.

First Edition

CONTENTS

ARIZONA ARGONAUTS

CHAPTER I

TWO PALMS

PIUTE TOMKINS, sole owner and proprietor of what used to be the Oasis Saloon but was now the Two Palms House, let the front feet of his chair fall with a bang to the porch floor and deftly shot a stream of tobacco juice at an unfortunate lizard basking in the sunny sand of Main Street.

"That there Chinee," he observed, with added profanity, "sure has got this here town flabbergasted!"

"Even so," agreed Deadoak Stevens, who was wont to agree with everyone. Deadoak was breaking the monotony of an aimless existence by roosting on the hotel veranda. "I wisht," he added wistfully, "I wisht that I could control myself as good as you, Piute! The way you pick off them lizards is a caution."

Piute waved the grateful topic aside. "That there Chinee, now," he reverted, stroking his grizzled mustache, "is a mystery. Ain't he? He is. Him, and that girl, and what in time they're a-doing here."

"Even so," echoed Deadoak, as he rolled a listless cigarette. "Who ever heard of a chink ownin' a autobile? Not me. Who ever heard of a chink havin' a purty daughter? Not me. Who ever heard of a chink goin' off into the sandy wastes like any other prospector? Not me. I'm plumb beat, Piute!"

"Uh-huh," grunted Piute Tomkins. "Pretty near time for him to be shovin' out as per usual, too. He was askin' about the way to Morongo Valley at breakfast, so I reckon him an' the gorl is headin' north this mornin'."

The two gentlemen fell silent, gazing hopefully at the listless waste of Main Street as though waiting for some miracle to cause that desert to blossom as the rose. At either side of the porch, rattled and crackled in the morning breeze the brownish and unhappy-looking palms which had given the city its present name. They were nearly ten feet in height, those palms, and men came from miles around to gaze upon them. It was those two palms that had started Piute Tomkins in the orchard business, which now promised to waken the adjacent countryside to blooming prosperity.

At present, however, Two Palms was undeniably paralyzed by the odd happenings going on within its borders. Contributory to this state of petrifaction was the location and environment of the desert metropolis itself. Lying twenty miles off the railroad spur that ended at Meteorite, and well up into the big bend of the Colorado, in earlier days Two Palms had been a flourishing mining community. It was now out of the world, surrounded by red sand and marble cañons and gravel desert and painted buttes; Arizona had gone dry, and except for Piute Tomkins and his orchard business, the future of Two Palms would have been an arid prospect.

Piute Tomkins was the mayor of Two Palms and her most prominent citizen, by virtue of owning the hotel and general store, also by virtue of owning no mines. Everyone else in Two Palms owned mines —chiefly prospect holes. All around the town for scores of miles lay long abandoned mining country;

the region had been thoroughly prospected and worked over, but was still given a tryout by occasional newcomers. The Gold Hill boom in particular had sent revivifying tremors up through the district, several unfortunate pilgrims having wandered in this direction for a space.

Inspired by the rustling quivers of the brownish palms outside his hostelry, Piute Tomkins had passed on the inspiration to other prominent citizens. They had clubbed together, and managed to get some wells bored out in the desert—installing mail-order pumping machinery to the indignation of Haywire Smithers, proprietor of the hardware emporium across the street. They then set out pear and almond trees, and sat down to get rich. Piute Tomkins had been sitting thusly for five years, and after another five years he expected to have money in the bank.

"I was wonderin' about them pears, when they come to bearin'," he reflected to Deadoak. "What we goin' to do with 'em when we get 'em? It's twenty miles south to Meteorite, and thirty mile west to Eldorado on the river, an' fifty mile north to Rioville. How we goin' to get them pears to market?"

"They come in an' buy 'em on the trees," said Deadoak encouragingly. It paid Deadoak to be heartening in his advice. He was the only man thereabouts who understood the workings of cement, and during the orchard boom he had put in a hectic six months making irrigation pipe. He also owned several mines up north.

"Speakin' o' that chink, now," he said, sitting up suddenly, "you say he's headin' for Morongo Valley to-day? I bet he's heard about that there mine o' mine—the one that stove in on Hassayamp Perkins an' broke his neck. Sure he didn't mention it?"

"He ain't talked mines a mite," said Piute, casting about for a lizard. "Nope, not a mite. Hay-wire was tryin' to interest him in them two holes west o' the Dead Mountains, but he plumb wouldn't interest in nothin'. It's my opinion, private, that he's aimin' to raise garden truck. Most like, he's heard of the irrigation projects around here—they was wrote up in the Meteorite paper last year—and he's come down to find the right place for garden truck. Chinks are hell on raisin' lettuce an' stuff."

"What in hallelujah would he do with it when he got it?" demanded Deadoak witheringly. "Eat it? Not him. Now, the way I take it——"

He hushed suddenly. The hotel door had opened to give egress to a large man—a tall, widely built man, clad in khaki—and a girl, also clad in khaki. The man moved out into the white sun-light, looking neither to right nor left, and vanished around the side of the building. His features, one realized, were those of a Chinaman.

The girl, who flashed a bright "Good morning!" to the two men and then followed, was slender and lithe, and carried over her shoulder a black case and tripod slung in a strap.

"Camera again," observed Deadoak, as she too disappeared. "Why in time do they go out workin' with that picture machine? It don't look sensible to me. Didn't you ask him?"

"Him?" Scorn sat in Piute's tone. "Tom Lee? He don't never talk. Don't know when I've seen a man that talked less than him. That is, in com-pany. Up in his own room I've heard him jabber away by the hour. Him and the girl always speaks English——"

"Say!" exclaimed Deadoak, excited. "I bet I got you now! You remember that guy come out three years ago an' boarded over to Stiff Enger's place by Skull Mountain? Lunger, he was, and his folks sent money for his carcass when he cashed in.

Stiff said that he'd stalk around by the hour talkin'
queer talk to himself and wavin' his hands at the
scenery."

"He was an actor, wasn't he?"

"Certain. Well, that's what this chink is—that's
why he's learnin' his parts up in his room! Then
he goes out in the desert somewheres with the girl,
and she puts him through his paces and takes pictures of him! Piute, I bet a dollar he's a movin'
picture actor and they're makin' pictures of him—
that's why they always go some different place!"

"Might be some sense to that notion," ruminated
Piute Tomkins. "Still, it don't look——"

From behind the hotel burst forth the roar of a
flivver. The car careened into sight, the big yellow
man sitting in the rear, the girl at the wheel. It
skidded into the dusty street, righted, and darted
away. At the next corner—the only corner—it
turned up past Stiff Enger's blacksmith shop and
disappeared.

"Uh-huh," commented Piute. "They're headin'
for Morongo Valley, all right, if they don't stop
somewheres first. They're plumb liable to stop,
too. That ain't but a track these days; no travel
atall that way. I told the chink it was a bum road,
but he just grinned and allowed the car could make
it."

"Well, there's scenery a-plenty up Morongo
way," averred Deadoak. "That's all there is,
scenery an' rattlers. Wisht they'd take a notion to
dig into that mine o' mine, they might dig up ol'
Hassayamp. He had a bag o' dust on him when
she caved in, but I reckon he's all o' twenty feet inside the hill."

Why Tom Lee had come to Two Palms, no one
knew. A most amazing Chinaman who spoke very
good English, who put up at the hotel and seemed
to have plenty of money, and whose business like

himself was a mystery. He would go for one day, or two or three into the desert, and invariably come back empty-handed, so far as anyone could tell.

What was even more astonishing, his daughter always drove him. At least, Tom Lee said she was his daughter, and she seemed quite satisfied. Everyone in Two Palms fairly gasped at the bare thought, however; for she was actually a pretty girl and looked as white as anyone. More so than most, perhaps, for life in Two Palms was not conducive to lily complexions, yet the desert sun had barely given her features a healthy sun-glow.

A pilgrim, during some prospecting toward Eldorado, had come upon the girl sitting in the car, one day, and had been struck dumb by sight of her. Later, he had wandered morosely into the Two Palms, begging a drink in charity, and murmuring something about having proposed mattermony before the ol' man showed up and he had realized the dread secret of her birth. Still murmuring, the pilgrim had wandered off toward Meteorite and had been no more seen of men.

"Still an' all," observed Deadoak, whose mind had reverted to this incident, "I dunno but what a man *might* do worse. She's durn pretty, I will say, and always has a right sweet word for folks. I dunno but what she might be glad to take up——"

"Now, Deadoak, you look here!" Piute turned in his chair and transfixed the other with a steely gaze. "I'm mayor o' this here town, an' deputy sheriff, and it's my duty to uphold morality and— and such things. Don't you go to shootin' off your mouth that-a-way, I warn you, legal! Don't you take too much for granted. We need irrigation pipe, and we're liable to need more, but that don't give you no license to presume. You go to outragin' the moral feelin's of this here community and somethin' will happen quick!"

"I was just thinkin'," Deadoak weakly defended himself. "And Mis' Smithers allows that she's a right smart girl, considerin' what's behind her——"

"Don't you think too hard," said Piute, getting up and shoving back his chair, "or you'll have a accident! Mind me, now."

He stamped inside the hotel, calling to Mrs. Tomkins in the kitchen that the guests had departed and she could tidy up the rooms a bit.

CHAPTER II

SHIPWRECKED MEN

SANDY MACKINTAVERS was slowly piloting his big Twin-Duplex along a rough and rugged road. It crested the bleak mesa uplands like a red-bellied snake. A twining, orderly road of brickish red, now and again broken into by flat outcrops of yellow sand or white limestone cut into its tires most pitifully.

One who knew Arizona would have recognized that road, although Sandy himself might have gone unrecognized. He was coated with the dust of several bathless days, and underneath the dust, his heavy features were drawn and knotted. Sandy had a general idea that he was in Arizona, but did not care particularly where he was, so long as the car kept going and he drifted westward, unknown of men.

Six weeks previous to this momentous day, Mackintavers had been a power in the world of mesa, ranch, and mine that centered about Albuquerque and Socorro; the world that he had now left far behind him to the eastward, forever.

His wealth had been large. His unscrupulous

fingers had been clutched deep in a score of pies, sometimes leaving very dirty marks about the edge. Mining was his specialty, although he was interested in trading stores and other enterprises on the side. Any bank in the Southwest would have O. K.'d the signature of Alexander Mackintavers for almost any amount.

Yet Sandy had few friends or none. His enemies, mainly those whom he had cheated or bluffed or robbed, feared him deeply. He gave no love to any man or woman. He was said to own the courts of the state and to be above the law; the same has been said of most wealthy men, and with about the same degree of truth.

For, of a sudden, the world of Sandy Mackintavers had cracked and smashed around him. Somewhere a cog slipped; he had been indicted for bribery. That had broken the thick crust of fear which had enveloped him, had released his enemies from the shackles of his strong personality. Overnight, it seemed, a dozen men went into the courts against him, backed by the evidence of those who had taken his money and had done his dirty work.

Sandy Mackintavers, for the first time in his life, had thrown up his hands and quit. His magic had gone; little things done in careless confidence now suddenly loomed up huge and threatening against him. He faced the penitentiary, and knew it; too many of his own hirelings had turned upon him.

Fortunately for himself, he slipped through the bribery charge on a technicality, and devoted himself to buying off his worst enemies. That saved him from the courts and the penitentiary, but it brought down upon him a horde of vultures—both men and women with whom he had in times past dealt with after his own fashion. Now they dealt with him, and in full measure.

Mackintavers was broken in spirit. Before he could rally, before he could get breath to fight, they crushed him with staggering blows on every side. Sins ten years old rose up from the past and smote him. He deserved all he got, of course. The vultures gathered around and stripped him to the bones, as pitilessly as he had stripped them in other days. His ranch, his mines, his trading stores—all of them went, one by one. When Sandy saw the last of his wealth vanishing, with more vultures hovering on the horizon and not a soul sticking by him, he climbed into his big car, the last remnant of prosperous days, and "beat it."

At forty-eight he was beginning life over again, with most of his nerve gone, at least temporarily, and a beggarly five hundred dollars in his sock. He had no idea of what might happen to him next, so he buried his wad in this first national bank and started.

With this brief digression, we find Sandy Mackintavers at the wheel of his big car, aimlessly crawling over the bleak mesa toward no place in particular. In the rear of the car were heaped a camping outfit and Sandy's personal baggage. Mackintavers knew that he was already far away from Albuquerque and his usual haunts, and well on the way to California; but he had no definite city of refuge in mind, unless he were to strike down across the border into Mexico. He had a hazy notion of selling his car somewhere, and then—well, his brain was still too staggered to be of much value to him. He was as a man dazed, awaiting the next blow and caring not.

When Mackintavers observed two men on the road ahead of him, he slowed down. He had lived thirty years in the Southwest, and he believed in giving men a ride, even if they were tramps, as the blanket-rolls showed.

"Ride, boys?" he sang out, slowing down between the two men, who had separated.

"You bet!"

The man to the left, a tall, rangy individual, hopped to the running board and opened the tonneau door behind Sandy. An instant later, Mackintavers felt something cold and round pressed into his neck, and heard the stranger's drawling speech.

"Sit quiet, partner, and leave both hands on the steering wheel—that's right. Now, Willyum, investigate our catch."

Mackintavers glanced at the other man and found him to be a rough-jawed individual, who was nearing him with a grin. Across the haggard, pouched features of Mackintavers flitted an ironic smile.

"What's this—a holdup?" he inquired calmly.

"Exactly," answered the cultivated voice behind his ear. "The owner of so highly pedigreed a car as this one, must perforce need his loose cash far less than Willyum and I. We are, I assure you, rank amateurs at the holdup game; this, in fact, is our initial venture, so be careful not to joggle this revolver. Amateurs, you know, are far more irresponsible with a gun than are professionals."

"You needn't be wastin' time and breath on *me*," said Mackintavers. "If there was any money to be made in your business, I'd join ye myself. Ye'll find eight dollars and eleven cents in my pockets, no more."

"Hold, Willyum!" ejaculated the bandit in the rear. "Let us engage our victim in pleasing discourse. Is it possible, worthy sir, that you do not own this fine motor car?"

"I own it until I meet someone who knows me," said Mackintavers grimly. He had none too great a sense of humor—one contributing cause of his downfall. But he knew that his five hundred was reasonably safe, since the average car driver does not carry money in his sock.

"There's something familiar about the shape of your head," observed the bandit in reflective voice. "I cannot presume to say that we have met socially, however. May I inquire as to your name?"

Mackintavers hesitated. He was warned by a vague sense of familiarity in this man's voice, yet he could not place the man or his companion. However, he felt fairly confident that they were not former victims, and concealment of his identity would in any case be futile.

"My name's Mackintavers. Aiblins, now, ye've heard of me?"

The hand holding the revolver jumped. The bandit slowly withdrew his weapon, and made a gesture which held his companion from entering the car to search the victim.

"Mackintavers!" he repeated. "Why, sir, we have read great things of you in the public prints! I am glad we had your name, for we could not rob you—on two counts. First, there is honor among thieves; second, you are a repentant sinner. We have read in the papers that you have devoted your entire fortune to reimbursing those whom in past years you have dealt with ungenerously. Sir, I congratulate you!"

Mackintavers winced before the slightly sardonic voice. It was true that the newspapers had pilloried him unmercifully; they had joined in the landslide that had swept him away, and their tongues had cut into him deeply.

"Who the devil are you?" he rasped, with something of his old asperity. "You talk like a fool!"

The bandit laughed. "Mr. Mackintavers," he said gaily, "meet Willyum Hobbs, formerly known as Bill Hobbs! At one time a famous burglar and safecracker—I believe the technical term is 'peterman'—Willyum was some time ago converted to the paths of rectitude. His present lapse from virtue is due solely to hunger. Willyum, meet Mr. Mackintavers!"

Hobbs grinned cheerfully and stuck forth his hand. He was a solemn man, was Hobbs, a very earnest and unassuming sort. It was rather difficult to believe him a criminal. Also, Bill Hobbs had his own ideas about society, being a well-read man of a sort.

"Glad to meet yuh," exclaimed Hobbs beamingly. "Say, that's on the level, too! I mean, about us bein' empty. I gotta admit it don't look honest to be stickin' yuh up, but gee! We had to do somethin' quick! We been on the square until now, the doc an' me."

"The doc!"

Mackintavers turned about, a sudden flash in his cold eyes, to meet the quizzical regard of the man in the tonneau.

For a moment the two gazed silently at each other. The bandit was not an old man, being distinctly young in comparison with either of the other two; yet something had seared across his face an indefinable shadow. It was a rarely fine face, beneath its stubble of reddish beard. It was not the handsome face of a tailor's advertisement—it was the handsome face that is chiseled by character and suffering and achievement.

Despite its harshness, despite the cynical eyes that sneered through their laughter, this red-headed man was a flame of virile strength and surging energy—tensed high, nervous, like steel in temper. The blanket-roll across his shoulders swung like a feather. His hands, as his bronzed face, were lean and energetic, unspeakably strong. It was evident that this man and Willyum had come from the very antipodes of life and environment. An overwhelm-

ing surprise lighted the broken face of Mackintavers as he gazed.

"The doc!" he repeated slowly. "Why—why—
aiblins, now—man, ye can't be the same!"

"I am, Mackintavers; the same man who removed that broken appendix from your insides two
years ago in St. Louis, and a thousand dollars from
your pocketbook for the job. Quite a drop for me,
eh? Quite a drop for Douglas Murray, to be a
bindle stiff, eh?"

Mackintavers stared, as at a ghost.

"I can't believe it!" he said. "Aiblins, now, it's
some joke—some damned nonsense! Why, you
were one of the finest surgeons in the country, a man
at the top, not yet thirty——"

Bitterness seared itself across the face of Murray.

"That's exactly what broke me," he asserted in
biting tones.

"But I don't understand!" blurted Mackintavers.

Willyum Hobbs made a gesture, an imploring
gesture; across his homely, earnest features flitted
a look of appeal, of anxious worry. He glanced at
Murray as a dog eyes his troubled master, with
love and uneasiness. But Douglas Murray laughed
jeeringly, harshly.

"Come, Mackintavers, look alive! It was success that downed me—too much work. I had to
keep going twenty hours a day to save human lives
during the influenza epidemic. It started me working on dope. I knew better, of course, but thought
myself strong.

"The dream book got me at last, like it gets all
the fools. One day, in the middle of an operation,
I broke down. I had to have a shot quick, and I
got it. I had to do it openly, if the man on the table
were not to die; so I did it. Inside of a week, the
news had spread through the whole city.

"It spread everywhere. I made an effort to fight, of course; did my desperate best to conquer the dream book. In the end, I won the fight, but by that time my nerve was gone. Everyone passing me in the street knew that I was a dope fiend. It was whispered at me socially and financially—from all quarters. At last I woke up to the fact that my money and good repute were gone. I can still practise medicine—if I have the nerve."

"Hm!" grunted Sandy. "Why didn't you stick it out? Aiblins, now, a man like you!"

"Why didn't you stick it out yourself?" Murray's laugh bit like acid. "Do you know why I stood in the top rank of surgeons? Because a great surgeon must be like a sword; he must decide instantly, quick and true and sharp—and he must be right. The hemming and hawing kind never reach the top, Mackintavers. And I—well, my nerve was gone after the publicity, and all. I was a branded man! Like yourself."

Mackintavers shivered slightly. "You haven't lost your nerve," he retorted, "or you would not admit it so readily."

"Rats! I've been on the road for six months, trying to recuperate under the open air and get away from everything. Now, Willyum! Roll a cigarette and don't shake your head at me. You'll like Willyum, friend Mackintavers. He has a proprietary interest in me. He believes that I restored some of his vitality——"

"Aw! you knows it damn well!" broke out Hobbs affectionately, and turned to Sandy. "He found me layin' in a ditch, and he cut me open an' took care o' me——"

"Oh, hush your babbling!" snapped Douglas Murray. "Let's discuss more pleasant matters. Where are you going from here, Mackintavers? You offered us a ride, you know——"

Sandy made a vague gesture. He could not have been recognized as the Mackintavers of a month ago; he was pitifully broken and indecisive.

"Anywhere," he said weakly. "Into Mexico—anywhere. You'd better hop in. We'll go on to California, huh?"

There was silence to his invitation. Hobbs was rolling a cigarette, Murray produced a briar pipe and raked up some loose tobacco from his coat pocket. He was sitting on the equipage in the tonneau of the car. The broiling sun of Arizona drifted down upon them, insufferable and suffocating.

"We're not broke," said Hobbs suddenly. "We're not broke, but we gotta get to grub quick. That's why we stopped you. This desert——"

Mackintavers waved his hand. "I have some grub back there. And a little money hidden. Let's go together, eh?"

Murray lighted his pipe and glanced at Hobbs, inquiringly, his eyebrows uplifted in a satirical questioning. Hobbs frowned in his earnest fashion.

"Why, Mackintavers, you and us has met up kinda queer; we're all in the same boat, sort of. But I dunno about goin' on together. I'm tellin' you straight, we gotta eat, but we aim to do it on the level—far's we can."

"You—what?" blurted Sandy. "You hold me up, and then you——"

Douglas Murray intervened.

"What Willyum is attempting to express," he said blithely, "is a simple, but profound thought. He has been a burglar; he is now reformed, and I trust is ambitious of leading an honest life. As for me, I have no particular ambition, unless it is to win a fairly honest place somewhere at the back of the world, and a chance to explore the anatomy of unfortunate humans. The idea, as you will gather, is that while we are shipwrecked men like yourself, we are essentially honest in our endeavors. We, at least, have no illusions. If we rob, it is from the necessity of remaining honest men at heart. You relish the paradox, I hope! It is really excellent.

"But how about yourself? I would not insinuate that we are better men than you, heaven knows! However, if you are about to enter upon a career of rapine and plunder, my dear Sandy, our ways had best separate here——"

Sandy Mackintavers, his head sunk upon his breast, made a gesture as if demanding peace. He stared out at the desert road, his fingers tapping the steering-wheel.

"You're a queer pair!" he reflected aloud. "Aye, a queer pair. To tell ye the truth, now, d'ye know what's broke me? It's because I've not a friend to my name. And why not?"

Murray spoke, with the cold, clear analysis of a vivisector.

"Because there's been no honesty in you. Sincerity is what makes friends."

"Aiblins, yes. They've taken my money— they've been afraid of me; when the pinch came, they turned on me and sank their fangs. And I've come to know what I've missed. D'ye mind, now, I'd like fine to have a friend or two!"

In the voice of Mackintavers, in his sunken face, there was the tragic wistfulness of a lost child seeking the way home.

"I would that," he pursued slowly. "Now, I could start clear again—if a man can ever start clear of his past. Can he? I dunno. I've always admired ye, Murray, and the way ye handled me that time in St. Louis; I've never forgotten it. To think that here ye are, to-day! 'Tis a queer world. Shipwrecked men, like ye say, and we're driftin' wild. Well, I've tried the other way, I've fought wi' the wrong weapons. If ye say the word, Murray, I—I'll start clear again!"

Murray knocked out his pipe and motioned to Willyum Hobbs.

"Hop in here, Willyum; I believe the grub is underneath me. Drive on, comrade!"

"Where to?" demanded Sandy, wonder in his eyes.

"Follow the road! Follow the path of ambition, to California. Let us find a town at the back of the world, and carve out our destiny from the desert sands!"

The starting gears whirred. The big car gathered momentum and drew onward along the blazing road that wound snakily across the scorched mesa land. The shipwrecked men were on their way to nowhere.

And Bill Hobbs burgled a can of tomatoes with gusto.

CHAPTER III

BILL HOBBS ARRIVES

SANDY MACKINTAVERS had a very definite reason for guiding the Twin-Duplex in the direction of Meteorite, at the end of the railroad spur that runs north from the main line and the highway.

The three partners had decided—or rather, Sandy and Douglas Murray had decided, for the vote of Willyum was always that of Murray—not to go on to California, and not to cross the line into Mexico. It was too hard making a living in California, and it was too hard to keep alive in Mexico. Their decision was to seek a one-horse town at the

back door of things, and there to seek a general re-
cuperation of spirit.

In order to do this with the proper degree of un-
concern, it was necessary to sell the big car and to
buy a flivver that would negotiate anything once.
Meteorite was a live town and was the headquarters
of a stage line which would undoubtedly use the
Twin-Duplex, so Sandy headed north to Meteorite

Thus did destiny weave her gossamer net.

"This is no place to settle down!" Douglas Murray wrinkled up his thin nostrils at the oil tanks and
the dump heap which fringed Meteorite. They
were arriving late in the afternoon. "This is an
abode of filth—a commercial metropolis!"

"It's a good place to start from, ain't it!" quoth
Willyum, gazing afar at the blue peaks rimming the
horizon. "Once we could get out in them hills—
aw, look at the colors on 'em! Wouldn't it be
great to camp out there?"

Sandy smiled grimly at the wistful ignorance of
the ex-burglar.

"I've done it in hills like 'em," he said, "lookin'
for color of another kind, and I've been glad to
drink the water out o' my radiator! Aiblins, now,
we'll find what we're looking for, beyond Meteorite.
Don't know much about this country."

It was four o'clock when they purred into Meteorite and drew up at the hotel—where was also
the stage headquarters. The travelers were hot,
dusty, and thirsty. Directly across the street from
the hotel, was a flaring soft-drink parlor, its depths
cool and inviting.

"Good!" exclaimed Douglas Murray, as he felt
the hot sand beneath his feet. "Come on over to
the liquid emporium, boys, and I'll set up the
drinks!"

"Not me," Sandy grimaced. "That sort o' stuff
gets my innards, Murray. Besides, I'd better be

seein' about business right now.   Aiblins, we might
make a deal to-night and be gone to-morrow."

"Suit yourself," Murray shrugged.   "How about
you, Willyum?   Ice cream or business?"

"Me fer the cold stuff," averred Bill Hobbs.
"I'm dry."

"Come on, then.   You register for us, Sandy?
Thanks.   We'll be back and join you shortly."

"Need any money?" volunteered Mackintavers,

"Nope.   Not yet.   We're far from broke,
thanks."

Murray and Hobbs walked across the street, stiff-
legged with much riding, and entered the alluring
portals of the refreshment palace.

A single man leaned over the bar, slowly con-
suming a bottle of near-beer and talking with the
white-aproned proprietor.   He was a dusty man,
a withered, sun-browned, sand-smitten specimen of
desert rat, and was palpably the owner of the two
burros tethered outside the entrance.

"Ice cream," ordered Murray, ranging up alongside the prospector.   "Have a dish, partner?"

"Thanks," rejoined the other, nodding assent.
"Sure.   As I was sayin', Bill, it was the gosh-will-
ingest thing I ever struck!   Think o 'me purposin'
mattermony, right off the bat like that—and a
good-lookin' girl, I'm sayin'!   And when she was
feelin' around for the right words to accept me,
prob'ly meanin' to fish around an' make me urge
her a mite, I seen her ol' man come walkin' along.
In about two shakes I seen he was a chink."

"Yes?"   The proprietor tipped Murray a wink,
and set forth the ice cream.   "What then?"

"I faded right prompt," said the desert rat.
"Right prompt!   I dunno—it kind o' dazed me fer
a spell.   When I got into Two Palms next day, I
was tellin' Piute Tomkins about it, and he up an'
says them two was stayin' at his hotel—the chink

and the girl, which same bein' his daughter, he allowed it was all right an' proper. I judge Piute was soakin' them right heavy, else he wouldn't ha' stood for chinks boardin' on him. Piute has his pride——"

"And he got a pocketbook likewise," put in the proprietor. "I know *him,* I do! Piute would skin his grandmother for a dime. What's the chink doin' over to Two Palms?"

"Damfino," rejoined the desert rat. "Piute don't know, an' if he don't, who does?"

"Where's Two Palms?" inquired Murray, who had been absorbing this information with interest. "Near here?"

"Near and far," said the proprietor.

"Near in mileage, but far in distance, so to speak. It ain't nothin' but a waterhole at the back door o' creation. Ain't goin' there, I hope?"

"Heading that way," said Murray. "What's there?"

"Well they got a bank, or did have, unless she's broke by now; and a hotel and a few other things. If I was you I'd go somewheres else."

"Where?"

"It don't matter particular—anywheres."

Murray grinned.

"You seem to have a down on Two Palms, partner. What's the idea?"

"Well, they's a close corporation there, a bunch of oldtimers that's mostly related and don't take much stock in outsiders, if you savvy. Nothin' there but desert. Stage runs up there once a week with the mail, which same if it wasn't contracted for wouldn't go."

"What's this about the chink and the girl?" put in Hobbs. "Sounds queer."

"If you ask me, it is queer!" said the desert rat, with some profanity to boot.

"They come through here, I remember 'em,"
spoke up the proprietor, leaning on the bar.
"Darned pretty girl, too. Mebbe he's *mining.*"

"Piute said not."

"Oh!" exclaimed Hobbs quickly. "Are there
mines around Two Palms? Gee! Say, doc, let's
get us a mine!"

"Might do anything," said Murray sardonically.
"Want to find it or buy it?"

"Buy it!" exclaimed Hobbs with fervent intona-
tion. "Sure, buy it! Let Sandy do it; don't he
know all about them things? Let's go on to Two
Palms an' do it!"

Murray nodded and turned from the bar. "Well,
so long!" he said in farewell, and sauntered out into
the street. Hobbs followed him.

The desert rat gazed after them with bulging
eyes; then, shoving the remainder of his ice cream
into his mouth, he drew the back of his hand across
his lips and left the place hurriedly. Disdaining
to notice his burros, he shuffled up the street to the
post office, entered, and bought a postal. Over
the writing desk in the corner he bent awkwardly,
and indited a laborious message to one Deadoak
Stevens, at Two Palms.

"There!" He gazed upon his handiwork with
great satisfaction. "If this yere intimation don't
git Deadoak to work, it'll be funny! They got the
coin, them three pilgrims has—look at the car they
rode up in! I bet I done Deadoak a good turn.
If I had a decent hole o' my own, now, I'd unload
on them birds!"

Sandy Mackintavers, meantime, had fallen to
work with true Scottish thrift; when the others rejoined him in the hotel, he was displaying the Twin-
Duplex to the proprietor of the stage line. The
latter gentleman exhibited very little interest in the
proposed deal, and disclaimed any notion of buying

the car; however, he crawled into her, over her, and under her, then summoned one of his drivers from the group of loafers on the hotel veranda and ordered him to drive the car around and bring her back.

In five minutes the driver returned, and violently disparaged the car so far as stage use was concerned.

"Well, I'll tell ye, now," said the owner, "I really ain't got much use for her. But I got a couple o' flivvers over in the garage, last year's model, good shape; if ye'd consider a trade and take 'em both off'n my hands, we might talk turkey. Step in the office, gents."

They stepped in, and presently stepped out again. Sandy had rid himself of the big car, attaining two flivvers and five hundred cash.

That evening he did a thing which would have mightily astonished anyone who had known the old Mackintavers. He called the other two into his room, and laid upon the table all his worldly wealth.

"Now, partners," he stated, "there's all I got. Split it up and start even."

Murray's keen eyes swept his face, and read there a stubborn earnestness. It was not without an effort that Sandy had achieved this moment.

"Aw, hell!" broke out Hobbs. "Wot kind o' guys d'you take us for, Mac?"

"We're partners, aren't we?" affirmed Sandy. "Aiblins, now, one friend ought to help another and——"

"We're more than partners, Mac," said Murray quietly. "We're friends, as you say. Is it your proposition that we throw all we have into a common fund?"

"Just that," said Mackintavers doggedly. "Each one of us helps the other to get on his feet, eh?"

"And use the common funds for that purpose?

I get you." Murray puffed a moment. "Well, Willyum, say your mind!"

"I say, Yes!" spoke up Bill Hobbs eagerly. "Mac's playin' on the level with us, ain't he? Well, then, meet him square. If all of us is goin' to be pals we——"

Murray made a gesture of assent, and reached under his armpit.

"Willyum was a hobo when we met," he said. "and hobos go heeled, Mac. I didn't leave St. Louis bone dry myself. Here's our contribution. We'll each drive a flivver from here, and if I were you, I'd convert this wad into travelers checks before we leave in the morning. They'll be good anywhere."

He opened a flat purse and drew out a roll of bills. Mackintavers gasped as they fell on the table. His features slowly purpled.

"Good gosh!" he ejaculated. "Why——"

"Nine hundred," said Murray. "Evens up pretty well with your thousand. You keep the bank, Sandy. Say, there's a place north of here called Two Palms, with an interesting yarn attached regarding a chink and a girl; smacks of mystery. Also, it's a mining country and little known. Let's go there to-morrow!"

"All right," said Sandy brokenly. "You—you boys now, how d'ye know I won't beat it with your pile? What right ye got to treat me——"

"We're friends and partners, aren't we?" cut in Hobbs. "Forget it, Sandy—forget it! Us guys is goin' to hang together, that's all. We're usin' your flivver, ain't we? Well, that's all right. If you see a chance to buy a mine, buy it; we'll be partners. If doc sees a chance to cut a guy open an' make some money, we're partners. If I see a chance to—to—to——"

"To crack a safe?" suggested Murray whimsi-

cally. Hobbs gave him a glance of earnest re-
proach.

"Aw! Come off o' that, Doc; well, whatever I
see a chance to do, we'll do. Right?"

Mackintavers nodded, and raked the money together.

A fact which the desert rat had foreseen, but
which hardly appeared to Murray as any momentous factor in the affairs of destiny, was that on the
following morning the stage went to Two Palms
with the mail.

A few hours after the stage pulled out, the two
flivvers were filled with the necessary elements and
crated tins of spare gasoline; Sandy Mackintavers
piloted one in the lead, and Murray and Bill Hobbs
followed in the second.

The road to Two Palms was good, comparatively
speaking; that is, it was a road. Before noon,
Sandy paused to lower the top of his car. Bodily
discomfort meant nothing to him; and he was more
used to sun than to wearing a hole through stout
imitation-leather with the top of his head, to say
nothing of the risk of breaking his neck.

"You bob around like a cork in a washtub, Mac,"
observed Murray. "When you hit that dry wash
a mile back——"

"Don't mention it!" grunted Sandy. "I forgot
which way the gas throttle worked—it's different in
an automobile. Why didn't we bring some lunch?"

"Too much interested in Meteorite scenery," said
Murray. "Willyum! Peter a can of something
—if 'peter' is the correct expression——"

"It ain't," retorted Hobbs cheerfully, "but I
will."

A frugal luncheon disposed of, they continued
the journey northward. That eighteen miles or so
to Two Palms, was longer than any fifty they had
previously experienced.

Meteorite lay among the hills, and in order to get to the basin which encompassed Two Palms, the road twined endlessly through the sandy washes and graveled valleys of the bleak red hills. They encountered the stage on its return journey, and had to back fifty feet to a turnout, a proceeding which was nerve-racking in the extreme.

But at length the sandy desert basin unfolded before them, and Two Palms in all its glory. It was not unlike a score of other desert towns they had encountered; a string of adobes and unpainted frame structures, crouching chameleon-like upon the sand, with wagon tracks in lieu of roads winding away to north and west. Drawing closer, the pilgrims discerned the details of Main Street, with its hitching posts and straggling fronts; the hotel, notable by reason of its twin palms; the hardware store, the general store and post office, the blacksmith shop at the corner; the long, low chain of roofless adobes where in more prosperous days Mexican workmen had lived; the abandoned newspaper office, the little group of men and women in the shade of the hotel porch, watching the new arrivals. And, hardly to be observed, was the figure of Deadoak Stevens, off to one side, with the fragments of a small-torn postal about his feet and a look of eager secretiveness in his eyes. Deadoak was thankful that he had grabbed that postal before Piute, as postmaster, had a chance to read it; having read, he had promptly destroyed the secret, and meant to garner to full harvest of these pilgrims unto himself.

Douglas Murray failed to observe a slight raise in the road which Sandy had negotiated with ease; his thoughts were all upon the hotel and group of live human beings ahead, and the correct manner in which to stop his car. Thus, he killed his engine a hundred feet from the goal.

"Curses on the beast!" he ejaculated, and crawled out. Bill Hobbs was ensconced in the tonneau.

Murray cranked—and then something happened. He remembered afterward that he had forgotten to brake the car in neutral. He remembered it after the radiator hit him over the ear and one of the fenders gently pushed him twenty feet distant.

Bill Hobbs sat on top of the load, paralyzed with terror, as the car leaped away. From the watchers on the hotel porch burst yells of grateful delight over this break in the monotony of existence. The flivver plunged at the nearest hitching post, blithely carried it away, and decided to investigate the abandoned print-shop.

When Murray sat up and wiped the sand from his eyes, he ruffled up his red hair and stared amazedly. The flivver was there, to be sure; one wheel had burst in the door of the printing office, the other was wedged about the steps, and the machine was lifeless. But Bill Hobbs had vanished. Unforeseeing the sudden halt of his equipage, he had shot headfirst from his perch, and neatly catapulted into the open doorway.

Murray was the first to reach the spot, while from the hotel porch streamed the others.

"Willyum!"

"Comin' right up," answered the voice of Bill Hobbs, and the latter showed himself in the doorway, grinning. "I've busted up somebody's place and——"

"Don't worry about that, stranger," said Deadoak Stevens, at Murray's elbow. "It ain't been occupied since Jack Haskins cashed in. He left a sister back east, but she ain't seen fit to remove the remains yet. Glad to meet ye, gents! James Cadwallader Stevens is me, but Deadoak Stevens by preference an' example."

"Meet Bill Hobbs, Deadoak." Murray waved

his hand toward the rumpled figure in the doorway, and turned as Sandy and the others joined him. "And this gentleman is Sandy Mackintavers, mining expert of parts East, who expects to settle here as Bill Hobbs has settled. I am Douglas Murray, doctor of medicine and surgeon extraordinary——"

Piute Tomkins hastened to rescue matters from the unseemly grasp of Deadoak, and performed the introductions with gusto.

"As mayor of this here municeepality, gents," he concluded, "I welcome you to our midst. Two Palms is on the crescent curve to prosperity an' wealth. The population is increasin' daily——"

"Say!" broke in Bill Hobbs, wrinkling up his face earnestly. "What's that you guys say about this here printin' office? There's machines and stuff in here—don't nobody want it?"

Piute waved his hand.

"There is no printer in our midst, pilgrim. All this flourishin' place needs is a real newspaper, but so far fate——"

"I'm it!" exclaimed Bill Hobbs gleefully. "I believe in signs, Doc—us guys was sure guided here! I'm goin' to take over this joint where I landed!"

Murray looked up at the ex-burglar. "You! Why, Willyum, I didn't know you were a printer or——"

"I ain't," said Willyum earnestly, "but I will be. Is it agreeable to you guys?"

Piute Tomkins bowed his lank figure. "Stranger, set right in the game! Them chips are yourn." He turned to Murray, caressing his mustache mournfully. "But, Doc, I'm right glad to welcome you to our midst, only we don't need no internal investigator in these parts, seein' that nobody ever dies here except by sudden accident——"

He paused, stared over Murray's shoulder, and his grizzled jaw gaped.

Down the street came a flivver, swaying and roaring—a dusty flivver containing no one except the girl at the wheel. She halted the car with a grind of brakes, and, seeming quite oblivious of the strangeness of the scene before her, leaned out.

"Mr. Tomkins!" she cried, an anxious excitement in her face. "Does anybody here know anything about medicine? My—my father has been hurt and——"

"Praise be to providence!" orated Piute quickly. "Miss Lee, meet Doc Murray—Doc, meet Miss Lee! I'm sure glad the good name o' Two Palms has been saved this-away—you'll make a livin' here yet, Doc——"

"Get in, please!" exclaimed the girl, with a swift gesture to Murray. "You'll have to come with me at once——"

"With pleasure, madam." Murray bowed, recovered his battered hat, and climbed into the flivver. The engine roared; the car crawled off, got its second wind, and vanished around the corner of the blacksmith shop on two wheels, Sandy and Bill Hobbs staring blankly after it.

CHAPTER IV

SANDY INVESTS TWICE

THE coming and departure of the girl was dramatic enough to leave all of assembled Two Palms transfixed with astonishment, until Piute Tomkins gave vent to his feelings, forgetful that Mrs. Tomkins and Mrs. Smithers were present. The indignation of Mrs. Tomkins at the language

of her spouse quite absorbed the attention of Piute
pro tem., and in this brief interval Deadoak Stevens
got in his thoughtful work.

Sandy Mackintavers caught a murmur at his elbow and turned to find Deadoak addressing him in
lowered tones.

"You're the mining gent, ain't you?"

"Aiblins, now," hesitated Sandy, "ye'll not consider——"

"Tut, tut!" exclaimed Deadoak, winking. "I
understand things, pardner; a friend o' mine over
to Meteorite sent me word that two gents were on
rout here with a minin' sharp. Now, let me warn
you not to give ear to these here desert rats all
around, but step over to one side with me. I got a
confidential communication——"

"Keep it, then," said Sandy brutally, "until we get
settled here! Come up to the hotel to-night."

"And ye won't talk mines to nobody else first?"

"Nary a soul," returned Mackintavers. "Hey,
Hobbs! You goin' to come out o' that place?"

Bill Hobbs scratched his head and considered his
position.

"If you guys will drag the corpse out of the way,"
and he gestured toward the flivver. "I'm goin' to
give this joint the once over, Mac. Join you over
to the hotel later. Gee! You ought to see this
joint, Mac! Where did Doc go to?"

Willing hands removed the flivver from the doorway. Deadoak, being rebuffed by Sandy, remained
to scrape an acquaintance with Bill Hobbs and elucidate the kidnapping of Murray; while Piute Tomkins, taking in hand his guest, performed the same
office to Mackintavers, en route to the hotel.

That evening, Deadoak sidled cautiously to Mackintavers's room, knocked, and slid inside as the
door opened.

"Ah!" he exclaimed, breathing more freely.

"Ding my dogs, but I had a stiff time eludin' that pirootin' son of a gun, Piute Tomkins! He suspects somethin'."

"So do I," said Mackintavers, grimly eyeing his guest. He did not know that Deadoak had just come from a long and involved conference with Piute, wherein property had changed hands and other arrangements had been made; he did not need to know all this, however, to realize that his visitor had not come for philanthropic purposes.

Deadoak, blissfully unconscious that he was introducing a new game and a cold deck to the gentleman who had invented that game and patented the cold deck, sank into a chair and blinked solemnly at the lamp.

He produced a battered corncob pipe, filled and lighted it, then straightened out his legs along the floor and blew a cloud of smoke.

"If I had money," he prologued dismally, "I wouldn't ask odds o' no man——"

"Me the same," struck in Sandy. "Aiblins, now, I'd wager there ain't a man in this country who couldn't develop a promising hole if he had money. Go ahead."

Slightly daunted by the grimly sophisticated front of his host, Deadoak took a new pull at his pipe and began afresh.

"It's a right queer yarn, this story I got on my mind," he observed dreamily. "Up north of here is the Dead Mountains, and it's a good name. If there's anything deader'n them hills, I'd admire to see it! Ye go out the good road along to where Piute an' me has got pear orchards an' wells. After that, it ain't no road—it's an excuse. I don't reckon anybody has traveled that way sinct ol' Hassayamp Perkins got stove in by the cave-in."

"How long ago?" queried Sandy seeking facts.

"Two year. I ain't been that-a way myself, and

nobody else ain't got right good reasons for doin'
it, except that there crazy chink. He went that-a
way this mornin', and he ain't got back yet.   Another hill fell on *him* I reckon. After ye get
through the marble cañon, there ain't only volcanic
ash and rock till ye come into the basin.   I been
over in Death Valley an' the Aztec Fryin' Pan, and
they don't hardly show up alongside that basin to
speak of. It ain't big, however, and from there ye
go into Morongo Valley."

"Sounds lively," commented Mackintavers without great interest.

"It is. If ye take two steps in any direction,
there comes such a buzzin' ye can't hear a man shout
at ye twenty feet away—that's how many rattlers
there is! Well, as I was sayin', Hassayamp homesteaded Morongo Valley. It ain't but a few hundred acres, and he'd located a spring o' water big
enough for all he wanted—he didn't wash much,
Hassayamp didn't."

The shaggy brows of Mackintavers were bent
upon the speaker in a silent but forbidding fashion
that somehow discouraged the careful narrative
which Deadoak had built up in his mind—a narrative with cunning discursions and excursions. He
decided to throw it all overboard and to reach the
point at once.

"As I was sayin', Hassayamp homesteaded that
valley to keep out other folks——"

" 'Twouldn't protect his mineral rights," shot in
Sandy shrewdly. "Mineral rights belong to the
state. Did he homestead the valley an' lease the
mineral rights?"

"I was comin' to that if ye give me time," said
Deadoak plaintively. "Yep, he done so. Reg'lar
five-year lease. Now, Hassayamp was Piute Tomkins' father-in-law by marriage, savvy? Well,
when the shaft fell in and wiped out Hassayamp,

Piute fell heir to the homestead, which same had
been proved up all correct, *and* the mine."

"Piute owns it now, then?"

"He do. I'm comin' to that if ye give me time.
But here's somethin' Piute don't know! A spell
before Hassayamp got stove in, he come to town
needin' money. Piute Tomkins, whose repytation
for pinchin' the eagle into a sparrer ain't laid over
by no one this side o' Phoenix, didn't have no faith
in him; but I did. So Hassayamp comes to me,
quiet, and gives me samples an' eloocidates how he'd
got a road up to the mine and had rigged up a hand
crusher and done other work there, and needed
money to see her through. I give him five hundred an' took out a mortgage on the hull prop'ty."

"Homestead   and   minerals?"   queried   Sandy
casually.

"Certain! I took in everything, you can bet!"
Deadoak tapped his pocket.

"You got the papers to prove it, of course?"

"Comin' to that if ye give me time. Ding my
dogs, ain't you got no patience? Well, me an'
Piute don't hitch extra well. After Hassayamp
cashed in that-a way, Piute always figgered on takin'
over the place, but he never got time. I figgered
on takin' it over, but never got around to it, rightly,
so let her drift. Piute don't know yet that I got
that mortgage, which same can be foreclosed any
time a-tall, it bein' two year old. So I got her
sewed up plumb legal, ye see."

"I see." Sandy's shrewd eyes narrowed. If
there was anyone in the Southwest who knew mining
law down to the ground, it was Sandy Mackintavers.
"What's in the mine?"

"Ding my dogs! I'm comin' to that now. Hassayamp got gold there—struck a lode o' quartz that
runs about twenty-five to the ton and promises to
get richer quick. Here's the samples he brung me."

Deadoak had now reached the apex of his elaborately conceived edifice.   Producing a buckskin bag, he emptied it on the table.   Specimens of very average gold quartz littered the table.   Among them were several pieces of a reddish crystalline substance.

"That don't look so bad," commented Sandy, fingering the quartz.   He indicated the glassy red samples.   "What's that stuff?"

"Volcanic bottle-glass, I reckon—how it come with the samples I dunno, unless Hassayamp thought it was pretty.   This here quartz, like you say, ain't bad; I'd say it was pretty dinged good, if ye ask me!"

Sandy's eyes glinted at the red-glass specimens, and suspicion filled his heart.

"Uh-huh," he grunted.   "What's your proposition?"

"Well, I don't want to sell outright.   That there lode is goin' to pay big when she's developed.   Looks to me, the way them specimens shape up, like she'd run into rotten quartz an' free gold; ye can see that for yourself.   Sooner'n sell the hull thing, I'd hang on a spell longer.   But here's my idee: You an' your pardners buy the mortgage an' give me a one-fourth int'rest in the mine.   You'll have to foreclose the mortgage——"

"Is it recorded?"

"Sure—I recorded her after Hassayamp cashed in an' Piute got his title."

"Uh-huh."

"Bein's you'll have to settle Piute, an' develop her an' so forth, I ain't aimin' to stick ye none.   Say, you buy the mortgage for five hundred, go ahead an' foreclose her, keep the homestead if ye want it, and give me one-fourth int'rest in the mine.   Ain't that fair?"

Sandy frowned thoughtfully.   He knew that on

this basis he was going to be stuck somewhere—and
he believed that he knew exactly where. Deadoak
was trying to unload upon him a worthless mortgage. Since that mortgage covered the mining
rights and the improvements thereon—property of
the state and not subject to mortgage—the docu-
ment was illegal.

Mackintavers had made a fortune because he
knew men, could probe into their minds and mo-
tives, could find their weak points and utilize them.
He had lost that fortune because he had tackled
the wrong man, and he had no intention of repeating
the mistake. He sized up Deadoak for exactly
what that gentleman was—a shiftless desert rat
planning to take in the innocent stranger, without
any very deep or well-laid plot. It aroused all the
predatory instinct in Sandy. Forgotten were his
virtuous resolves and high aspirations. Before his
mind's eye unfolded a simple but beautifully perfect
scheme by which he might grab this property entire.

Being tempted, he fell. He could not well be
blamed, for those red-glass samples on the table,
those carelessly lumped pieces of "volcanic bottle-
glass," showed the richest ruby silver Sandy had
ever seen outside Nevada!

Sandy had already weighed the possibility of
those samples not having come from Morongo Valley; he had decided that they had done so. He was
staking his game now upon his judgment of Deadoak Stevens, who was palpably a weak stick.
Swiftly weighing things, he decided that Deadoak
was trying to rid himself of a worthless mortgage
upon an ignorant stranger. And having so decided,
he gambled.

"Aiblins, now," he said at length, "I'll tell ye!
Want to look over the ground first, ye understand.
I'll give ye ten dollars cash for that mortgage, and
my note for the balance, ninety days, includin' in the

note that the title is clear except for this mortgage, and that the samples ye got there come from this mine in question."

"A note?" exclaimed Deadoak in obvious dismay. "Why, I was figgerin' cash——"

"Well make the note thirty days, then.   I ain't buyin' a mine from a set o' samples!"

"Oh, that's fair enough, I reckon," said Deadoak. "Sure, fair enough.   You can pick up that lode five minutes after ye get there, and match up them samples with the outcrop!   That quartz sticks out o' the surface, Mac!   If Hassayamp hadn't got ambitious to strike the rotten streak, he'd ha' been rich now."

"Where's the nearest State Land office?"

"Meteorite—that's the county seat, too," replied Deadoak, entirely unconscious that Sandy wanted that bit of information very, very badly.   "Here's the mortgage—it ain't a mortgage, it's the other thing, the one that lets ye grab a place the minute payments ain't made, with no legal notice or nothin'. I had a cousin oncet that cleaned up a lot o' money over in California, usin' them things instead o' mortgages, so I used it too."

Deadoak handed over a much thumbed but entirely legal deed of trust.   Mackintavers inspected it carefully, then calmly jotted down the details as to the location of the defunct Hassayamp's property.

"Aiblins, now," he said, rising, "I'll just run down and see Piute Tomkins' deed to that property— make sure it corresponds with this location, and is clear otherwise.   Ye don't mind, o' course?"

Deadoak looked up in weak protest, then yielded.

"O' course not," he said with dignity.   "Bein' a stranger, it's natural that ye should take precautions; but when ye've been here a spell, ye'll find out that——"

"Ain't doubtin' you," said Sandy.   "Not a mite!

Now, you write out that note to suit yourself, but make it contingent upon the facts bein' as you say. And write out a conveyance o' that mortgage to me."

Leaving the room, Mackintavers slowly descended the stairs toward the office, where Piute Tomkins and Haywire Smithers were engaged at their nightly cribbage. He paused on the landing, to chuckle to himself.

"This mine is comin' cheap!" he reflected. "Volcanic bottle-glass—that's a good one! Aiblins, now, it's a gamble. Should I do it to-night or wait? If Deadoak had paid the least attention to the ruby silver—but he didn't! Not a mite. He was all afire over selling me that mortgage. I'll do it!"

He went on down stairs. His whole scheme of action, which promised to work with the beautiful precision of a machine, demanded that he conclude the deal to-night and get Bill Hobbs off to Meteorite within the hour. Reaching the hotel doorway, he saw a bobbing light across the street in the newspaper office. His voice lifted in a bellow.

"Bill Hobbs! You there?"

"Want me?" came the reply. "Is Doc back? I been lookin' over this joint——"

"Get over here in a hurry. I need you."

Sandy turned to the office, where the two cribbage players were gazing up at him. He jerked his head slightly to Piute.

"Can I see ye a moment in private?"

"Certain, certain!" Piute rose with almost suspicious alacrity. He had been waiting and praying for just such an invitation. "Step into the back office, will you?"

When the two men were alone in the inner office, with the lamp lighted and the door closed, Sandy Mackintavers brushed aside all preamble and came direct to the point. He held in his hand the deed of trust, which he had not returned to Dead-oak.

"I understand ye have a homestead in Morongo Valley. I'll offer ye a hundred cash for it." Pi-ute's leathery complexion changed color.

"A hundred!" he repeated in injured accents. "Why, that there homestead is the very pride an' joy of my heart! She sure is. I aim to lay out pears in that there Valley next Jan'ary. Got water, she has——"

"Here's a mortgage on the property," and Sandy brutally tapped the paper in his hand. "I've bought it. It's two years old. Sooner than foreclose, I'll buy your title. Aiblins, now, ye have a price?"

Piute looked a trifle staggered, but shook his head firmly.

"Nope. Nothin' under a thousand takes that there place! I dunno 'bout this mortgage—ain't heard of it——"

"Look at it," struck in Sandy. "I'll go to law and take the place if I want! Give ye two hundred cash, not a cent more."

"Nope," said Piute, bristling. "I got a few rights my own self, and I know 'em! If it's the minerals ye're after——"

"Minerals!" exclaimed Mackintavers with scorn. "I'm done with mining. I want a homestead."

"Well," proposed Piute, "that's diff'rent. I'll give ye an option on the homestead for a thousand. Ye look her over, and if she's what ye want——"

"Nothing doing," rejoined Sandy. "I'm offering cash down, here an' now. And I won't listen to a thousand."

Piute hesitated. He had not glimpsed Sandy's roll of travelers' checks, these three pilgrims looked none too prosperous, and he began to think that he had set the ante too high.

"Tell ye what," he said, "I wa'n't figgerin' on sell-ing, but cash is diff'rent. And this here mortgage thing—well, say seven hundred!"

Sandy thought of that ruby silver ore, and fished for his check book.

"You show me clear title an' give me a deed, and I'll give you five hundred. Take it or leave it! That's the last word out o' me."

"All right," said Piute.

Mackintavers signed up checks to that amount. Bill Hobbs arrived in time to join Haywire Smithers in witnessing the transfer, then accompanied Sandy to the upstairs room where Deadoak awaited them. Hobbs was mystified, but Sandy refused explana-tions.

"I brought Mr. Hobbs along," said Sandy, "as his money will be partially concerned. Aiblins, now, if you've got the note and conveyance made out——"

"Here they be," said Deadoak, trembling with concealed joy.

Mackintavers read over the papers carefully, while Deadoak explained the situation to the be-wildered Bill Hobbs.

"Ten dollars cash—here ye are," said Mackin-tavers. He signed the note and returned it with a ten-dollar bill. "When Doc Murray gets back, we'll go out and look over the place."

"Suits me," and Deadoak sidled to the door. "Good luck, gents! See you later."

Left alone, Sandy Mackintavers pressed Willyum into a chair and set forth exactly what he had ac-complished. He took up the samples of ruby sil-ver ore.

"I never saw anything to beat that ore—any-where!" he said. "And these desert rats never heard of such a thing; all they know is gold. Can ye run a flivver, Bill?"

"I can't," said the bewildered Hobbs, "but I guess I can. Why?"

"You got to run back to Meteorite to-night—right now!"

"Gee!" breathed Willyum, his eyes bulging. "What's the rush?"

"Shut up and listen!" roared Sandy. "Aiblins, now, ye think I'm a fool. Well, I'm not! If a minin' lease ain't worked, it lapses; if proper reports ain't made, it lapses; if it's mortgaged, with improvements, it's illegal. Deadoak's deed o' trust ain't worth the paper it's written on, and he knew it!"

"But—but you bought it——"

"I gave him ten dollars as a free gift. That note, now—when he comes to collect, he'll get nothin'. But I got hold o' the mortgage to save trouble, that's all."

"You ain't goin' to pay the note?"

"Not hardly!" said Sandy with a grim smile. "My property will all belong to you an' the doc. I guess I can trust you men with it! Now, I bought Piute's deed in order to have clear title to everything. Savvy?"

"Not—not yet," murmured Willyum dazedly. "Who owns the mining rights?"

"The state! The lease has lapsed long ago, and ain't been renewed. I'm goin' to write out a bill o' sale, givin' you an' Doc all I own, so Deadoak will have nothin' to sue on when he presents that note. After he's out o' the way, we'll settle things. You beat it for Meteorite right off, and when the land office opens in the morning—be there! Take out a mining lease on this entire Morongo Valley homestead land—in your own name. Get it for five years, under the precious metals clause. I'll convey the mortgage to you. Record that in your own name and let her go. We don't need to foreclose

on that worthless paper.   It simply clinches everything in our name, clear."

"But listen! Wait till Doc comes home and——"

"Wait for nothin'!" shouted Sandy furiously.
"Aiblins, now, d'ye know what this Deadoak scoundrel will do? He knows as well as I do that his
mortgage is illegal.   About to-morrow night he'll
be in Meteorite expecting to lease mining rights on
that valley, meaning to stick us later on.   Savvy
that?"

"How d'you know none of these guys ain't done it
already?" asked the worried and still bewildered
Hobbs.

"I'm gambling on their general shiftlessness.
Men of that stamp, not expecting us to arrive and
not expecting me to buy the place without seeing it,
will think they have lots of time to work the double
cross.   Now, ye'd better run some gas out o' my
flivver and fill up your own tank."

"But this—this ain't on the square, is it?" protested Bill Hobbs weakly.

"On the square!" repeated Sandy, stifling his own
doubts with a ferocious mien.   "Of course it is!   I
bought a worthless mortgage with a worthless note
—ain't that even?"

Bill Hobbs declined to struggle further with the
problem, and gave up.

Meantime, Deadoak Stevens was closeted below
stairs with Piute Tomkins in the inner office.   Deadoak was just pocketing two hundred and fifty dollars.

"Fall for it?" said Deadoak.   "Piute, ding my
dogs if he didn't fall clear through the crust and he
ain't stopped yet!"

"Well, we got a good price, I'm bound to admit,"
said Piute thoughtfully.   "As a beginning, it's good.
But I'm a bit worried over them minin' rights, Deadoak.   If we'd knowed a couple o' days ahead that
them pilgrims was on the way, we could ha' renewed

the lease or took out a new one. You got to tend
to that pronto."

"Yep," agreed Deadoak. "I'll take that cayuse
o' your'n and ride over to Meteorite in a couple o'
days. Then I'll lease them mineral rights. Might's
well try to shave that note over to town, too; mebbe
somebody will know who Mac is."

"Don't wait no couple o' days," said Piute sagely.
"You light out on that cayuse 'fore daybreak!
When them pilgrims gets tired o' lookin' for ruby
silver in that there prop'ty, they'll most like go to
workin' Hassayamp's gold lode. Then we trots
out the minin' lease on 'em, with threats o' prosecu-
tion for workin' without no lease."

"She listens good," and Deadoak nodded.
"Ding my dogs, Piute, if I ain't sure glad them pilgrims come to Two Palms to-day!"

"I'm sure glad," corrected Piute, "that we
knowed they was coming! But I wisht we'd
knowed it a few days earlier. I didn't allow they'd
bite so quick an' sudden, without even lookin' over
the place. Them ruby silver samples was what
done it."

"Them," admitted Deadoak modestly, "and the
way I played my hand."

"Well, you get them rights, and get the lease
sewed up quick!" admonished Piute. "But don't
advertise it none. Go to the newspaper office and
stick a piece in the paper about them wise men from
the east alightin' in Two Palms an' buyin' property
reckless and regardless. Say the printin' office was
sold for two thousand, and Hassayamp's homestead
for five thousand, and there's a big boom comin'
this-a-way——"

"But, Piute," protested Deadoak, "they'll know
we're plumb liars, them Meteorite folks will!"

"They know it anyhow," and Piute Tomkins
grinned as he closed his safe.

CHAPTER V

CLAIREDELUNE

DOUGLAS MURRAY, sitting beside the unknown girl as she drove out of Two Palms,
was for a moment dazed by the face of her. With
Koheleth, Murray had sworn that all was vanity
and an empty chasing after winds; yet the very sight
of this girl's face, anxious and smitten as it was with
hurried fear, for a space struck the cynicism from
him.

"You're a real physician?" she asked, her eyes
not lifting from the road ahead.

"I am, madam; Douglas Murray, at your service. I arrived in Two Palms about ten minutes
ago, and from what I have seen of the place, I do
not wonder at your astonishment."

"Oh—I remember now! There were automo-
biles there." She flashed him a sudden, swift
glance, then returned her gaze to the road. "My
name is Claire Lee. My father has been hurt—
we had a puncture, and while I was fixing it, he
wandered off on the hillside. I think he fell. After I got him back into the car, he fainted, and he
looked so terribly ill that I stopped at the first op-
portunity to leave him in the shade, and managed to
get him there. The road is so rough that I thought
it would hurt his leg——"

"Very well done," said Murray quietly. He
wondered what kind of a man her father could be,
to let this girl fix a puncture. "The road is pretty
bad, beyond a doubt. Was his leg broken?"

"I don't know. I was so afraid—I thought it
might have been a rattlesnake, but he said no——"

Something in the way she bit off her words hurriedly and anxiously, struck Murray as out of the

ordinary. He dismissed the query as he studied her face, feeling a little in awe of its startling and indefinable beauty. Despite its quietly poised strength, despite the upflung chin, its every line was carven with a rarely delicate precision. Each contour was mose exquisitely balanced. The hands and fingers, too, revealed this same fine artistry of line.

In her face lay character, strong and sensitive; no whit out of drawing, as Murray would have expected to find in a girl of the desert places. Only in her eyes lay a deeply indefinite shadow, a hint of rebellious pride, expectant, as though ready to take up arms instantly against some dogging trouble-maker. The sheer beauty that shone from her clearly level blue eyes and veiled her pale, sun-golden skin, was about her like an evanescent gossamer substance, striking her lightest word into shiftings of lost meanings and half-sensed sweetness.

"Clairedelune!" thought Murray. "Clairedelune—lady of the troubadours, sweet lovehurt of the soul—dear spirit-fragrant whiteness of the silvern moonbeam in the fairy ring! Clairedelune—embodied ecstasy of the poet's soul, the light that never was on land or sea——"

A sardonic curve tipped his lips as the flivver bucked and reared and cracked his brow against its top.

"Oh!" exclaimed the girl penitently. "I'm sorry! I always do the wrong thing with this car. I've just learned to drive it, and it's so different from a Twin-Duplex! I always open the throttle when I mean to close it."

So she had been driving a Twin-Duplex! The more Murray studied her, the more her presence here puzzled him. Wealth and breeding—even in the lines of the khaki dress was the one, and the other lay in her eyes.

"You've not been long in this country?" he asked.

"No, we came from San Francisco." She checked the words abruptly, as though she had spoken before thought. Then, perhaps finding it necessary to avoid abruptness, she added: "And I broke the plate-holders when I got father into the car—just as we thought we had succeeded! That means it must be done all over again."

"Taking photographs, eh?" Murray laughed whimsically. "It seems to me, Miss Lee, that you could take photographs anywhere in this country and they'd be all the same!"

"Oh, no indeed! We've been looking for a particular place—well, no matter. There's where father is."

She pointed ahead to a patch of green and brown. This was Piute's so-called ranch—a frame shack beside the road, with a few young Lombardy poplars sprouting into the sky, and acres of young pears stretching symmetrically across the desert floor. The dull clank clank of the pumping engine reverberated ceaselessly. No one lived on the place, but Piute Tomkins came out twice a week and had the engine going during these intervals, for irrigation purposes.

Experiments of some kind, thought Murray; that explained it very well. The father was a scientist engaged in work here, no doubt.

Murray thought at first that the road ended here; then he saw that it continued, an indefinite track winding away over the blazing, sun-white desert surface, winding between outpost yuccas, across to the horizon of this level expanse, as level as a billiard table, swept and garnished by the desert winds.

"Oh, he is conscious—and watching us!" exclaimed the girl as she halted the car.

Murray leaped out. In the scant shade under the poplars, beside the road, lay the figure of a man, shoulders and head propped up by his rolled-up coat. His open eyes were fastened upon Murray as the latter approached.

It was with a distinct mental shock, almost a physical shock, that Murray realized this man was a most unmistakable Chinaman. Then, for the first time, he remembered the tale of the desert rat in Meteorite.

So he understood now the shadow in the girl's eyes—yet, he swore to himself that there must be some tremendous error of providence here! He did not look back at the girl; he gave his whole attention to the matter in hand. He heard her voice speaking his name, and saw the man before him make a quiet gesture of acceptance. Then Tom Lee spoke.

"My left leg, doctor. The knee is hurt. The pain is severe."

Murray saw now, that the strong, masterful, yellow features were beaded with the sweat of pain. He knelt, then glanced up.

"A knife, Miss Lee? I shall cut these trousers to avoid causing further suffering———"

It was Tom Lee who silently reached into his pocket and produced a knife, which the girl took and opened, handing it to Murray. The latter fell to work.

For ten seconds, the slender, powerful hands of Murray busied themselves about the injured member; a scant ten seconds, touching lightly and deftly. Then from Tom Lee broke a low, tensioned grunt of agony. His fingers clenched at the ground, his head fell back into the arms of the girl. He was senseless.

"Oh!" she cried out. "What is it—what have you done———"

Murray rose. The old sardonic twist was in his face now as he looked upon them. Still the clear beauty of the girl drove into his heart; the fright-

ened, wondering face of her was like a sweet hurt
to the soul.

"A dislocated knee," he said quietly. "I have
replaced it. Perhaps we had better lift him and
place him in the car now, while he is unconscious.
A few days of repose will see him none the worse."

"There is nothing else?" she exclaimed. "But
you have not examined——"

Murray's brows lifted. "My dear young lady,"
he said drily, "more than one surgeon has been glad
to stand at my operating table and learn of my tech-
nique. In this case, I have both examined and oper-
ated; there remains only convalescence."

A slow flush crept into her face as she stared at
him. But she ignored his rebuke.

"Why—it was wonderful! A touch—only a
touch——"

Murray bowed. He had left his hat in the car,
and the late afternoon sun struck his coppery hair
to red gold.

"Thank you, Miss Lee," he said, and smiled
frankly. "I value that compliment more than many
I have received in other days. And now, may I
suggest that we lift him into the car at once? I
will take—or wait! There is a house of some kind
here; let us make him comfortable for the night.
You return to town in that car, and obtain some
more easy-riding conveyance. He is a large man,
and would have to sit doubled up; we could not get
into town before dark, and I would like to bandage
his knee properly without delay. An hour or so
might make a difference of days in his recovery."

"Just as you think best," she answered. "He
must recover as soon as possible——"

"I'll look around here."

As he sought the shack, Murray angrily shrugged
his shoulders. The discovery of the racial identity
of her father had left him dazed; now he revolted

inwardly against the fact. There was nothing good in the world after all. Beautiful as this girl was, exquisite as she was, she was a living lie—not by her own fault, perhaps, but no less a lie. For Murray, the world was tainted again.

He found the shack to be a one-room affair, containing two bunks with dubious blankets, a table, and two chairs. Behind it was a shed containing the clanking gas-engine, upon which he promptly put a quietus. Returning, he found Tom Lee still unconscious.

"Let us carry him. I'll take him about the hips —you take his shoulders."

Although he had perforce taken for granted her ability, Murray was a little surprised at the way in which the girl carried her share of the burden— lightly and with ease. Strength in that fragility, he thought!

When they had put the man in one of the bunks, Claire spoke quietly.

"If you'll wait here, please, I'll get some stuff for bandages."

He nodded, and sat down beside the bunk. He watched the face of Tom Lee curiously, and to his inward astonishment found himself reckoning it a very fine face. Here was not one of hybrid orientals who seeks notoriety by taking unto himself a white wife; in repose, the man's face was singularly massive, eloquent of self-repression, instinct with a firm command. Not a handsome face in any sense, but most striking. A man, thought Murray, who lived a stern inner life—a man who had mastered the secret of reserve.

"Here," said the girl's voice. Murray turned to her. She was extending several strips of silk and one of linen; her clear eyes spoke of anxious solicitude, but were unembarrassed.

"He has not recovered yet?"

"Thank you. These are excellent, Miss Lee! I'll have him fixed up in no time. No, I don't want him to recover just yet."

He was aware that she had again left the shack, but now he was bending over the man's figure, intent upon his task, bandaging the injured knee firmly and deftly. When at length he finished and sat back, he found that the liquid black eyes of Tom Lee were open and were calmly regarding him.

"Broken?" demanded the yellow man laconically.

"No; dislocated. You'll be around in a few days."

The massive chest heaved, as though in a deep breath of relief. The eyes flickered again to the doorway; following them, Murray saw Claire enter, a basket in her hand.

"Fortunately, we've some lunch left, Doctor Murray—oh!" She saw that Tom Lee was awake, and she hastened to the bunk, pressing her lips to the cheek of the yellow man. "I'm *so* glad it's nothing serious, Father! And wasn't it wonderful to find Doctor Murray——"

The big powerful hand of the yellow man patted her shoulder.

"It's all right, my dear," said Tom Lee, surprising Murray again by the perfection of his English. "No great harm done. The pictures are safe?"

"I broke them—getting you into the car——"

"Never mind." The yellow face was quite impassive. "Easy enough to get more, Claire. Why am I in this place, Doctor? And where is it?"

Murray explained to him in a few words. "I'll stop here with you, while Miss Lee goes in to town for a wagon or vehicle of some sort—even a buckboard might do. There's no great hurry about it. We're only a few miles from town, and I'd not advise moving you before the morning."

"Very well, Doctor," said the deep, grave voice.

"Suppose that you leave Claire with me, and you take the car into town. You'll find a thermos of tea in the car—we had an extra one that we did not use. If you'd not mind getting it, I think we can provide a very fair meal."

Murray nodded and passed out to the car. Upon reaching it, he saw what he had not previously observed—the rear of the front seat was fitted with a large carrying bag, and in the tonneau was an open camera case, from which had been disgorged half a dozen plate-holders, most of them trampled and cracked. The carrying bag was unstrapped, and from it Murray took a quart thermos bottle, then returned.

He found the table covered with the contents of the basket—sandwiches, tinned meat, and half a dozen odd little crocks filled with the most amazing Chinese delicacies. Tom Lee ate nothing, but smoked a tiny pipe of gold-mounted bamboo, which Claire filled and lighted for him. Nor did he talk at all, save to answer a direct question, leaving the burden of conversation to Murray and the girl. His eyes watched Murray sharply, however; perhaps he did not fail to note that while the red-headed medico was discreet enough to ask no questions regarding them, he also avoided all reference to himself.

"I expect to settle in Two Palms," said Murray suddenly, feeling that they were wondering about him even as he was about them. "For my health. I came here with two friends, and we may all become citizens of the desert for a time."

The girl's eyes went to her father, as though to seek from him permission to speak. But Tom Lee watched Murray through his pipe-smoke, and made no sign.

"It is a wonderful place," and the girl sighed a little. "Savage and——"

"Ah!" exclaimed Murray. "You must have blankets; these nights are cold.   You can't use these horribly soiled ones in the bunks, Miss Lee."

"There is a suitcase strapped behind the car," spoke up Tom Lee.   "Everything necessary is in it."

Murray went out to the car and began unstrapping the suitcase he found there.   The sun had fallen behind the western buttes—purple-red peaks that seemed to jut out of the level desert floor, solid blocks of shadowed Tyrian now, that with the sunrise would betray the most delicate of greens and pinks, and that with noon would gleam savagely in the harshest and crudest of stark reds.

And here the green pear trees, five-year trees, silvered the sunset-reddened sand as though reflecting the pale whiteness of the sky that would darken soon into the deep blue of the spangled night.   Murray paused and looked at it all, awed before the silence.   Then came a crunch of sand and a voice behind him.

"It is the magic hour of the desert—this and the sunrise, yet each so different!   I wonder that artists do not try to paint such things, instead of hills in the sun and the bald architecture of buildings!   Here is the miracle, and they see it not."

Murray turned to the girl.   "The miracle indeed, Clairedelune!" he said softly.

Her eyes met his, and she was laughing.

"That," she said unexpectedly, "is what Father calls me!"

"Oh!" said Murray, remembering suddenly.   How in the name of everything could a Chinaman pick upon such a name as that—a name of poetry, of romance, almost of oblivion!   A sudden distaste for that name seized upon Murray.

The girl read the sardonic thoughts in his face, and turned away.   A coldness was upon her when she spoke; as it were, a veil was drawn between them.

"If you'll bring the suitcase inside, please, we'll get Father fixed up comfortably."

Murray obeyed dumbly.

Half an hour later, he started for Two Palms. He should have covered the few intervening miles in no time, but one of his forward tires blew out with a roar and left him sitting thoughtfully in the mountain places.

By the time complete darkness fell, he had found a spare tube and was patching up the blown tire with fumbling fingers. Presently he got the stubborn rubber obedient to his wishes, and for fifteen minutes labored over a wheezing pump.

It was nearly midnight when he came laboring into Two Palms under the flooding moonlight, and with sighs of fervent relief brought his vehicle to a halt beside the dark and silent frame of the hotel.

"No, I guess I'll stick to the name," he thought, as he climbed out and gazed at the silvern glory of the night. "Clairedelune! Shall I let a big yellow man drive all the romance out of things? Not yet. Find the best that remains in your life, my boy, and transmute it into precious metal if you can; you need it! Well, it's been a strenuous day—I'm for bed. Time enough in the morning to organize the rescue party."

CHAPTER VI

DEADOAK FEELS REMORSE

HAYWIRE SMITHERS had at one time maintained a livery, which was now defunct. However, he disinterred an ancient surrey, hitched up

one of Piute's horses, oiled his springs, and set forth
with Murray to fetch in Tom Lee and Claire.

Before leaving town, however, Murray was inter-
viewed by Sandy Mackintavers, who laid bare the
little deal in real estate. Murray listened without
comment, his keen eyes searching the heavy features of Mackintavers.

"I thought," he said quietly, "that you had decided to throw overboard all the shady tricks of
yesterday, Sandy?"

Mackintavers flushed. "Shady? And what's
shady about this, will ye tell me?"

"Giving a note that you don't expect to pay, for
one thing."

"Wasn't the paper worthless that I gave it for?"

"No matter; it was unnecessary. That note will
be met and paid, Sandy."

"Man, ye don't understand this game!" said
Sandy with earnest conviction. "There was nothin'
wrong about it; one man get ahead of the other,
that's all! Aiblins, now——"

"Aiblins, now," and Murray smiled quickly,
"we're partners, so say no more about it. Only,
after this, let me in on these little deals, Mac; if I'd
been here last night, you'd not have given that note.
After this, we'll pull together—and go slow. I'll
wager that when Hobbs gets back, you'll find that
you've been neatly stung."

"How?"

"Lord, man, *I* don't know! I was merely express-
ing an opinion. We'll put the deal over, however,
and if Willyum holds to his notion of being a printer,
we'll give him a helping hand."

"Right."

So Murray went forth into the desert, and it was
nearly noon when he returned. The surrey dis-
charged its passengers at the hotel, and Tom Lee
was carried to his room. He had a slight touch of

fever and Murray assumed prompt charge of him, installing Claire as nurse and ordering that the injured man be kept alone and unexcited.

Luncheon over, and his patient reported asleep, Murray discussed immediate plans with Sandy.   To go out to Morongo Valley and investigate their purchase, was naturally the first impulse of both men; but they had to await the return of Bill Hobbs, in order to make sure of their position.   That Hobbs himself would accompany them to Morongo Valley, was unlikely.

"We may get off in the morning," said Sandy. "He'll not like it there, Doc.   He's taken a notion to the printin' business, and his heart will be back here."

"Let him stay here, then," assented Murray, "and go in for his chosen profession!   At least, for the present.   He'll get tired of playing by himself, I imagine.   Suppose we go over and get the shop cleaned up a bit for him?"

Sandy agreed.   On the hotel porch they encountered Piute Tomkins, who was busily engaged in hounding unfortunate lizards to a miserable fate. Murray paused and addressed him.

"As the mayor of this municipality and deputy sheriff, Mr. Tomkins, we call upon your aid!   Now is the time for all good men to come to the aid of the party.   Arise and shine!   If you want a print-shop opened here, let's go and open it.   Our estimable partner Bill Hobbs will be back anon, and upon his return he'll find the place cleaned up.   It will encourage him."

"Where's he gone?" queried Piute, untangling his legs from his chair and rising.

"Joy-riding.   Careening blithely forth upon the desert winds, his soul unblemished by care and his tires filled with ethereal zephyrs.   Comest thou?"

Piute looked a trifle blank, and followed.

The shop was just as the defunct owner had left it—or rather, as Willyum had left it the night previous. The neglect and dirt of a twelvemonth faced them, and they attacked it valiantly. After half an hour, however, they gave it up as a hopeless job.

"I never seen a clean printer yet," observed Piute thoughtfully, "and there ain't no use tryin' to improve on the Lord's handiwork, I reckon. I'm goin' to rest a spell."

He departed. Murray looked at Sandy, and grinned.

"Well, the floor looks cleaner, at least! Let's take an inventory!"

Sandy dismally shook his head and drifted away in the tracks of Piute. But Murray, who was operating with the interests and future of Bill Hobbs in view, continued his labors. He was enjoying himself, sating his archæological cravings, as it were. Having rescued Bill Hobbs from an aimless existence of more or less criminality, he felt that if Hobbs now had leanings toward settled life in this spot, he should be aided and encouraged thereto. Murray was not oblivious of a sense of responsibility; besides, he had a real affection for the earnest Willyum.

He explored the place thoroughly. Coming in from the outside world, in touch as he had been with the prices of things, he was astonished to find that the shop must have been well stocked up shortly before the demise of the late proprietor. The ink-rack was filled with tubes and tins; a gasolene drum reposed in the corner; news print paper was stacked high in a closet, ready cut, and there were two untouched rolls; bond and job paper of all kinds was in abundance.

The large foot-power job press seemed new and good, while the cutter and other varied machines

were in fair condition, type racks, furniture, stones
—all the paraphernalia of a printing establishment
were here. Murray was not so sure about the
press, and with reason. This was an ancient and
much mended relic, a flat-bed hand-power creation
such as made Ben Franklin famous; an instrument
such as is keenly sought after by dilettanti print-
artists who love good work, and shunned by those
who seek commercial results.

"Looks to me as though Willyum can step right
in and take hold," thought Murray. "He can learn
to set type easily enough—he'll have to! There's
a place to sleep in back, and he can rustle his own
meals. I guess Bill can manage."

Returning to the hotel, he took a chair beside
Piute and Sandy, and was talking idly when Claire
Lee appeared in the doorway.

"Mr. Tomkins!" she exclaimed. "How can I
get off some letters and telegrams?"

"Give 'em to me," said Piute. "Stage comes in
next week."

"Next week!" Dismay filled the girl's face.
"But—but these are important! They must go off
at once!"

Piute pulled at his mustache and frowned.

"Sho!" he exclaimed. "If I'd knowed that this
mornin', you could ha' sent 'em by Deadoak. He
took my hoss an' rode over to Meteorite."

Mackintavers gave Murray a significant glance,
followed by a wink.

"But surely," persisted the girl, "there must be
some way——"

"There is," said Piute encouragingly. "If ye
don't want to take 'em yourself in that car, why, I
reckon Shovelface Ryan would saddle up and ride
over for five dollars. He's the helper up to the
blacksmith shop. Shovelface done set off a blast
too soon one time and it plumb disorganized his

talkin' and hearin' apparaytus, but if Stiff Enger is around he can interpret for ye."

The girl hesitated an instant, then came out into the sunlight and walked up the street.

"It's right queer, now——" and Piute favored his auditors with an exposition of his own views, the views of Deadoak, the views of Haywire, and in fact the views of Two Palms in particular and in general, upon the subject of Tom Lee and Claire.

Before Piute had exhausted the subject, Claire came into sight again, returning. At the steps she thanked Piute for his suggestion.

"Mr. Ryan is going," she said, then paused. "Father is still asleep, Doctor Murray. Do you think he's all right?"

"Absolutely, Miss Lee," answered Murray. "He must be kept quiet for a few days, that's all. I'll look in on him tonight."

She nodded and was gone.

Conferring with Sandy, Murray decided to get one of the flivvers in shape for the trip to Morongo Valley, and ascertained the road carefully from Piute. That gentleman was openly curious as to the whereabouts of Bill Hobbs, but gained no satisfaction; and presently took his departure in somewhat of a huff.

"Aiblins, now," said Mackintavers, "we may take for granted that Hobbs will be back sometime tonight, so that we can start in the morning, if his report's good. Suit ye?"

Murray nodded. They took the car over to the hardware emporium of Haywire Smithers, and filled her with gasolene and oil; their spare cans were still untouched.

Claire joined them at the supper table with word that her father had awakened, and when his meal was finished, Murray went to visit his patient. He found Tom Lee taciturn, the fever departed, and mentioned that he would be gone for a few days.

"We've invested in a mine," he explained, smilingly, "and we're anxious to look the ground over. You'll need no attention, Mr. Lee, if you keep quiet. Three days in bed, and you'll be able to step around with a cane. I'll see you when I return."

"Very well," said Tom Lee without comment.

Murray went downstairs to find Bill Hobbs at the table, devouring everything in sight. Piute was hanging around, so the cautious Willyum made no reference to his trip, beyond stating the unavoidable fact that he had been to Meteorite. And at this, Piute Tomkins could not repress his uneasiness.

"Gee, that road was suttinly fierce!" remarked Willyum between bites. "I left there about noon, and had two punctures comin' over the rocks. Say, I met a guy on horseback, too! That guy Deadwood——"

"Deadoak!" said Piute explosively.

"Yep, Deadoak. He give me a hand blowin' up a tire."

Piute was looking very melancholy when the three partners left the dining room and adjourned to their own room.

Once in private, Bill Hobbs unbosomed himself of sundry papers. He had carried out his business, and he merely turned over his papers to Mackintavers with a grin. Sandy examined the documents, and nodded grimly.

"Good! D'ye mind, Murray, what our host said about Deadoak? Ye met him, Hobbs. He was on his way to Meteorite, to get the mining lease!"

"Oh!" said Bill. "Come to think of it, he did look kinda funny!"

Murray chuckled. "Then, Sandy we own everything in sight?"

"Everything," assented Mackintavers vigorously. "And a good job it is!"

"All right. You look dead for sleep, Willyum, so turn in. We're off in the morning to inspect the property. Want to go along?"

Hobbs hesitated.

"Well, I want to bad enough, only for that there joint across the street——"

"All right." Murray chuckled again. "We've cleaned up a bit for you, so fall to work! In two or three days we'll be back, and have an arrangement in regard to the future. If you're seriously set on opening up a print-shop, we'll agree——"

"As partners?" queried Willyum anxiously.

"Sure," asserted Sandy, with one of his rare smiles. "We go three-square in everything! Mine and homestead and newspaper—we'll be running the country next!"

" 'Where every prospect pleases and only man is vile,' " quoth Murray, and grinned. His grin was worthy the name, and was most reprehensible in a man of his years and experiences.

"You take the papers," said Mackintavers, extending them. "Don't leave 'em with Bill. 'Twouldn't be safe. A mere ex-burglar would be an infant in arms with these natives to plunder him!"

"I s'pose so," agreed Bill Hobbs mournfully, and bade his partners farewell.

At six in the morning, Murray and Sandy Mackintavers drove out along the north road toward Morongo Valley, and vanished for a space from human ken. At a later hour, Bill Hobbs went forth to his "joint," and was too much absorbed to show up again at the hotel until supper.

And, in the meantime——!

Toward noon, Claire summoned Piute Tomkins to her father's room, with word that Tom Lee wished to speak with him. Puite obeyed the sum-

mons.   When he entered, Tom Lee gazed at him
steadily for a moment.

"I wish to know, Mr. Tomkins," he said slowly,
"who owns the valley at which we looked the other
day—Morongo Valley, I think the name is."

"Who—who owns it?" stammered Piute.   He
was of a sudden acutely mindful of a sub rosa trans-
action by which Deadoak had transferred that property to him, and he to Mackintavers.   "Why—d'ye
mean the homestead or the mine, now?"

"Both," snapped Tom Lee impatiently.   "All
of it—all of the little valley!"

Piute was positively staggered.   He had no certain clue from this whether Tom Lee wanted the
mine or not; chances were, he did.   Murray and
Mackintavers were gone—and Bill Hobbs, he
guessed shrewdly, knew little of the matter, or at
least could sign away nothing.

"Well, I'll tell ye," said Piute, desperate.   "Right
queer about that there place, it is!   Ye see, the fel-
ler that homesteaded it an' worked the mine, he got
stove in under his own shaft.   My father-in-law, he
was, and a right mean ol' scoundrel to boot.   Well,
Deadoak Stevens, he wanted the prop'ty, on account
o' Hassayamp havin' a bag o' dust on him and meanin' to dig up the remains——"

"Who owns the property?" cut in Tom Lee impatiently.

"Why, Deadoak!" rejoined Piute.   "At least,
he done so a couple of days ago, and I reckon still
does."

"Where is he?"

"I dunno.   Went off to Meteorite yes'day.   He'll
be back soon enough."

"If you'll send him to me, Mr. Tomkins, I'll appreciate it greatly."

"Certain, certain," and Piute backed out, pausing
in the corridor to mop his beaded brow.   Tom Lee

had been to Morongo Valley and had found something. Mackintavers had been deluded into buying
the property."

"Plague take it!" said Piute. "If Deadoak was
here now!"

Late that night, Deadoak staggered into the hotel
and fell upon the neck of Piute Tomkins with tears
—metaphorically speaking. Curses were nearer
the truth.

"He done beat us to it!" sorrowed Deadoak, rolling a cigarette while Piute rustled him a cup of coffee in the kitchen. "He done grabbed the minin'
rights, Piute——"

"Let it go!" exclaimed Piute energetically. "Listen here, now——" He expounded the interview
with Tom Lee.

"That there chink has found somethin'!" he declared with vigor. "You chase up to his room an'
see if he wants to buy the place."

"Ding my dogs, Piute! *I* can't sell that there
place no more—she don't belong to me!"

"If he wants it, get an offer. If it's enough, buy
it back from Mackintavers!"

Deadoak protested. He was saddle-galled and
weary, disconsolate and disgusted, and he had no
heart for intrigue. Piute Tomkins goaded him
to it, however, and sent him despite protests to
the room of Tom Lee.

Fifteen minutes later, Deadoak stumbled downstairs to the office where Piute awaited him. He
dropped limply into a chair.

"Well?" snapped Piute.

"Ain't no well—nothin' but a dry hole," mourned
Deadoak. "That there chink offered—or rather,
I brung him up to offer—five thousand cash for the
place. Ding my dogs! If only we hadn't acted so
preceptous with that there pilgrim! I ain't never
knowed what real remorse was until right now——"

"Well, saddle up an' beat it to Morongo Valley pronto," exclaimed Piute. "Buy back——"

"Not me! I done had enough ridin' to last my mortal lifetime——"

"You're goin', and you're goin' in the morning!" asserted Piute emphatically. "Savvy? See what that there chink found—trail him down! I got no use for yeller men cheatin' honest citizens out o' their rights. You're goin', understand?"

Deadoak assented weakly that he understood. Presently, however, he rallied again.

"Now, Piute, show some sense!" he pleaded. "Ain't you jest said that the chink and this Doc Murray were out together? Well, they framed up the deal on us, that's all; the doc got the chink to——"

"You're a plumb fool, Deadoak," exclaimed Piute scornfully. "Why, the deal hadn't been put through when Murray went out to 'tend to the chink! 'Course, it might ha' been framed up since; all these here pilgrims seem a durn sight smarter'n you'd think for. I tell ye what——"

"Say!" broke in Deadoak with sudden remembrance. "I met Shovelface Ryan on his way to Meteorite—the chink girl had give him ten dollars to take some letters over there pronto. Tellygrams too. Well, Shovelface give me a squint at 'em, but he wouldn't let me open 'em a-tall; he's a queer cuss, Shovelface is, in some ways! Them letters was addressed to chinks in San Francisco, and they had photygrafts inside—they'd been put in damp and had curled up; I could feel 'em——"

"That proves it!" cried Piute in triumph. "That proves it, Deadoak! This here chink done located somethin' out to that place. And by whiz, he photygrafted it! Then he writ back to all his chink friends to let 'em in on the good thing." ·

"But all this," said Deadoak thoughtfully, "ain't nothin' to me no more. *I* don't own no mine in

Morongo Valley! I don't own nothin' except a
note for five hundred——"

"Well, *I* got some money to work with," broke in
Piute. "You vamose out to that there mine and
look her over! The chink an' the girl brung back
some pictures and some of 'em was broke, but I
guess a few was saved; the girl developed 'em in
that closet the chink hired for a dark room. Most
likely she left 'em there. I'll have a look in there
early in the mornin', and mebbe we can get a clue.

"Then, you chase out to the valley an' keep your
eye on things. Take some grub and a pair o' blankets, and watch what them pilgrims does, savvy?
Take them glasses o' mine, and you can lay up top
o' the hill all snug."

"The sun lays up there, too," said Deadoak,
plaintively. "It lays up snug, and it's hotter'n hell,
and brings out the rattlers an'——"

"You never mind," cut in Piute. "You're a-goin',
that's all!"

Deadoak bowed his head in bitter assent.

"My, but you're plumb sot in your ways, Piute!"
he returned feebly. "I'll go."

CHAPTER VII

STUNG!

SANDY MACKINTAVERS was desert-wise, so
far as automobile travel was concerned. He
did not travel without spare water-bags and lengths
of rolled chicken-wire, and at Meteorite he had
fitted his flivver with a running-board pump.

After passing the marble cañon and negotiating
the stretch of bad land where volcanic ash sifted
into the air and obsidian glittered under foot, Murray steered the flivver down into the basin where all

road was lost, where the loose sifting sands were blazing with the heat of an inferno, and where the car bogged down into the bottomless dust. Sandy deflated the tires, and when this would no longer serve, utilized the chicken-wire to run out of holes; by some miracle of desert sense, he managed to hold the right direction, although the rude map furnished them by Piute was useless to Murray.

It was nearly evening when they arrived at the spot dignified by the name of Morongo Valley, and the westering sun transmuted the sterile scene into one of glorious radiance and scarlet-tinged hues. All around stretched the peaks of the Dead Mountains, not clothed with the glorious forests of New Mexico, but with their naked eminences now gleaming in blue and scarlet fires of sunset, their valleys long streamers of darker purples, their bald slopes a yellow golden glory.

The valley itself was a box cañon, a small one, the upper end a solid mass of greenery. There was water here—a tiny trickle, that had been brought from the hillside to vivify the upper flat, and had given its precious life to all the higher slopes, before it lost itself in the farther sands.

The road, better preserved here, led them to the shack of Hassayamp. It was scarce worthy the name of shack—a rough erection of boards and scraps of tin, designed only to afford shelter from the elements. Sandy, standing beside the car and scrutinizing the hill-slopes, pointed upward.

"That's the mine, I'm thinkin'—that contraption o' timbers halfway up. It seems to have caved in. We're not interested in that, however; ruby silver is what'll make us sit up! Time for that in the morning."

Murray viewed the interior of the shack, and declared for sleeping in the open air.

They were up and about by sunrise. Murray

was cool and rather sardonic in regard to the whole
affair, but Mackintavers was cheerful and blithe as
any boy of a prospector on his first search for earth-
gold.   The sight of that glittering silver ore, that
wondrous ruby silver ore whose arsenic had ruined
many a man and whose silver content had made
thousands rich, was like a tonic in the blood of
Sandy.

By evening they had gone over the ridge wherein
lay the unfortunate Hassayamp, and had found no
ruby silver vein.   They had struck gold in promising lodes, but gold was naught before the ruby silver
—if they found it.   Sandy continued cheerful, and
Murray was coolly complacent, doing as Mackintavers bade him but frankly without hope of success.

With the following morning, they took picks and
labored valiantly until shortly before noon.   Then
Murray descried a little group of figures breaking
its way toward them—not from the direction of
Two Palms, but from the north, from the desert of
the Colorado.   The group resolved itself into two
plodding, patient burros and the nondescript outline
of a desert rat.   The latter greeted them as they
met him at the shack.

"Howdy, pilgrims!   Seen your smoke this mornin', and sinct I was headin' in for town anyhow, I
come this way.   My land, but you're in style, ain't
ye!   Autobile an' all—say, is that a real autobile?
I seen one oncet, las' time I was over to Eldorado
—but sho!   Here I be, forgettin' all decency!   My
name's George Beam, gents, though most folks ad-
dress me as Sagebrush."

"Glad to meet you," said Sandy cordially, com-
pleting the introductions, "and ye better sit in with
us for a snack, old-timer.   Any luck?"

"Ain't kickin' none," said Sagebrush, combing the
sand from his wealth of sodden gray whiskers.   His

eyes followed Murray. "Say, is them real bakin'
powder biscuits ye got? Well, I never! They
look real good, too, for them kind; I allus had a notion folks ought to study sour-dough more back in
the settlements, but mebbe there's somethin' to bakin' powder——"

Sagebrush drifted along garrulously, glad of a
chance to talk. Presently, when the coffee had been
finished and pipes were lighted, he gazed around
and grew personal.

"This here is a good place," he observed, "if it's
quartz you're after, gents. If it don't intrude none,
what ye lookin' for?"

Mackintavers chuckled, and produced his ruby
silver samples.

"This," he answered laconically. "Know it?"

Sagebrush took the samples, inspected them, and
then began to grin widely.

"Ruby silver!" he ejaculated. "Ye don't mean to
say—my gosh! Pilgrims, I'm right pained to hear
tell o' this, but——"

"Huh?" queried Sandy with a grunt. "What
d'ye mean?"

"Ye didn't allow them samples come from here,
did ye?"

"Understood so," returned Sandy, frowning.
"What d'ye mean, huh?"

Sagebrush grinned again. "Why," he said, heft-
ing the samples, "las' time I seen these here spec'-
mens, they was reposin' on the desk o' Piute Tomkins, back to Two Palms. Piute brung 'em home
from Tonopah three year ago, and was right proud
of 'em, too. I reckon that there no-account Deadoak pirated 'em from him and passed 'em off on
you. Deadoak is right smart, some ways——"

Murray looked at the gaping Mackintavers, and
rolled over with a shout of laughter.

"Stung, Sandy!" he cried, sitting up. "Hurray!

The bad man of New Mexico stung by a simple Arizona native—whoop! The biter got bit—oh, Sandy, Sandy! And look at the big blisters on my perfectly good hands——"

Sandy growled something inarticulate, then rose to his feet.

"I'm goin' to look at them quartz lodes," he grunted. "See ye later!"

Sagebrush gazed after him with sober mirth.

"Too bad ye got took in," he observed. "But I'm right glad ye take it calm, pilgrim. If ye didn't get bit too deep, ye got a fine place right here. Me, I like to git farther away from settlements—too many folks around spoil the desert. But if ye like this here oasis, she ain't bad. Say, if you're a doctor, wisht ye'd look at that there Jenny burro o' mine. She ain't been right peart for two-three days; kind o' down on her feed. Ye might light right on what she needed——"

Murray assented and strolled over to the burro in the train of Sagebrush. The whimsical irony of it struck him full; Douglas Murray, peer of the finest surgeons in the land, giving advice upon a sick burro! But he gave the advice, and grinned as he watched the aged desert rat shuffle off down the valley with his animals.

Sagebrush wended his way down the valley in patient tolerance of sun and sand. But of a sudden he wakened to the startling fact that his name was being called; amazedly, he peered up at the hillsides, shaded his eyes with his hand, and descried the figure of Deadoak Stevens approaching, carefully leading one of Piute's cayuses down the rocky descent.

An hour afterward, Deadoak was riding up to the shack in the valley, with a fine appearance of just finishing the end of a toilsome journey. A meeting with Sagebrush had afforded him a plan of campaign. He observed Murray sitting before the

shack cleaning a revolver, and dismounted with a
cheerful greeting; his cheerful expression vanished
quickly, however, when Murray pointed the revolver
at him and rose, blazing with wrath.

"So you've come to the scene of your crime, Deadoak! Put those hands up—that's right! And
stand still—don't back away; you've nowhere to
back."

"Wh-what's the matter?" stammered the paralyzed Deadoak.

"The matter?" repeated Murray. "You know!
You've defrauded honest men, and now you're going
to settle up. If you've any last words to say, say
'em quick! My finger's trembling on the trigger.
Tonight you'll be reposing under that tree; we're
here alone, Deadoak Stevens, and you shall perish
at the hands of the man whom you——"

Deadoak trembled, and his jaw sagged.

"Say!" he croaked. "I—I—honest, now, I come
out here to square things up! I heard that Mac
was lookin' for ruby silver—them samples was a
mistake! Piute said he'd put 'em in with Hassayamp's stuff one time. I rid here to——"

"What!" Murray lowered his weapon, in genu-
ine amazement. Deadoak leaped at the chance.

"Yep, that's right, Doc! *I* didn't go to defraud
nobody! If you ain't satisfied with the deal, I'll
take back the prop'ty and no hard feelin's—that's
what I rid out here to say, if ye give me a chance.
Ding my dogs, I ain't no gunman. P'int that thing
another way!"

Murray obeyed.

"You don't mean that you'll take back the property? At the price we paid?"

"Certain!" assented Deadoak, fervently virtuous
and hugely relieved. "Give ye a profit, if ye feel
bad. Why, Doc, we wouldn't go to pirootin' no pilgrims—future denizens o' this here great an' glo-

rious Two Palms! We wouldn't have ye feel that
we was anythin' but honest an' simple natives, wel-
comin' you to our midst. We'll go to 'most any
length to make things good. If we'd knowed that
Mac was attracted by them ruby silver samples—
which same I didn't know—we'd have run down the
thing then an' there——''

"Hold on," interjected Murray. "Here's Mackintavers now."

Sandy had descried the arrival of the visitor from
afar, and was now hastening toward the cabin. It
was a rare thing, an unknown thing, for Sandy Mackintavers to meet any man who had successfully bilked
him; he arrived upon the spot somewhat out of
breath, and gazed upon Deadoak more in sorrow
than in wrath.

Deadoak, however, hastened to avoid any trouble
by apprising Sandy of the reason which he avowed
had caused his visit.

"And now," he added, screwing up his leathery
countenance into sanctimonious lines, "I stand ready
to do the right thing, gents. I'm offerin', this bein'
on behalf o' me and Piute together, what ye paid for
the prop'ty and five hundred to boot."

"What about your mortgage?" queried Sandy
shrewdly.

"Include that in the takin' back if ye like. All I
want is to do the right thing."

"All right," said Sandy. "Murray, let me speak
with ye to one side."

Deadoak sat down and rolled a cigarette. Taking Murray's arm, Sandy mopped his face and
walked out of earshot, then he paused. As he met
Murray's puzzled gaze, an earnest look crept into
his heavy features.

"Ye'll leave this matter to me?" he queried. "In
other words, will you be willing to let me gamble
for the good o' the firm?"

Murray smiled quizzically. "Go as far as you like, Sandy! I'll back your play."

"And if we go broke on it, no hard feelings?"

Murray laughed and clapped him on the shoulder.

"Don't be a fool! We're men and not children. Play your own game!"

Sandy looked vastly relieved, then strode back to Deadoak.

"Well, now, your proposition is good," he said cordially, even genially. "I'm proud to meet a man like you, Deadoak Stevens! We thought you and Mr. Tomkins had trimmed us, and were inclined to be sore about it—now that we've found the mistake, we apologize."

"Then you take me up?" queried Deadoak eagerly.

"No."

"Wh—what! Ye said no?"

"Of course!" returned Sandy warmly, taking no heed of the thunderstruck look which had clouded Deadoak's staggered features. "Would we take advantage of ye that way? Not us! We're not that sort! We don't whine, Deadoak; we're not kids. We'll keep what we got, and make the best of it!"

Deadoak's countenance was a study in futility.

"You—d'ye mean——" he choked, then continued feebly. "Have ye found somethin'?"

"Maybe, we have!" Sandy beamed upon him. "Just between ourselves, friend, I'll tell ye that we have. So—ye see?" His wink was significant.

"I see," agreed Deadoak mournfully.

"'Twill make ye rejoice, no doubt," pursued Sandy, "to know that our luck was good. We appreciate your disinterested——"

"'Senough!" blurted Deadoak, turning. "I'll be weavin' back, I guess. So long."

"Won't ye wait till mornin', anyhow?" queried Sandy with concern.

"Nope, thanks."

Dejectedly, hopelessly, Deadoak stumbled to his cayuse, pulled himself aboard, waved a limp hand, and rode down the valley. He was slumped in the saddle like a man who sees no hope in the future.

"He's mighty cheerful over something," said Murray drily, and chuckled.

"Cheerful?"

"Well, Sandy, suppose you elucidate? Why did you turn him down?"

Sandy faced his friend and made a wide gesture.

"Murray," he said earnestly, "I'm playin' a hunch. Why should that fellow come here and make us an offer? I don't know—but there was something behind it. We've got something that somebody wants. And I've a notion who that somebody is."

"Oh!" Murray gave him a keen glance. "Then you really found something?"

Sandy rubbed his chin thoughtfully. "Come with me and I'll show you."

Murray accompanied him past the shack, up toward the head of the canyon. Sandy led the way to one side, where a high rocky wall formed a solid background. Before this was a stretch of sand, perfectly level, a hundred feet wide; this was enclosed on either hand by a low growth of manzanita, whose grotesque, wine-red limbs curled eerily in the sunlight.

"Look there," said Sandy, pointing.

On either side of this little clearing, a stake had been thrust into the sand. About the head of either stake, had been bound a scrap of red paper. One scrap had been torn away by the wind. On the scrap which fluttered from the other stake, was a flaring black Chinese ideograph.

"Aiblins, now," said Sandy, while Murray examined the paper, "that looks like a chink laundryman's mark, eh? And ye said that the chink, Tom

Lee, had been out here and was comin' home when ye treated his leg. What did he put those stakes in for?"

"I'll bite," said Murray, gazing at the scene with a frown of perplexity. "What?"

"Blamed if I know," returned Sandy.

CHAPTER VIII

DOCTOR SCUDDER

DAYS of honest work and virtuous toil evolved a new Bill Hobbs—a grimy individual streaked with sweat and daubed with printer's ink, yet as absorbedly delighted in his new task as a child with a fresh toy.

For the first time in his life, Willyum was his own boss at actual labor. The financial aspect of his travail had not yet arisen to trouble him. Naturally swift to comprehend things mechanical, he set himself to learn type, and succeeded more or less. He had found enough old job stuff set up to show him the use of the quoins, sticks, and furniture—although these names meant nothing to him—and after various attempts in which some type was sadly ruined, he managed to get the hang of the job press. The flatbed was a simpler proposition.

"Gee!" he observed, standing in his doorway one noon with a fine air of proprietorship, and watching the dusty stage roll in from the south. "Here's another stranger comin' to town. And the doc ain't back yet with Sandy! Well, I guess I'd better eat an' then begin to get out the first issue of the paper. We'll see who this stranger is, huh?"

He walked across to the hotel, where already most of Two Palms was assembling with avid curi-

osity to watch the debarkation of the new arrival.
Bill Hobbs took one square look at the stranger,
then he suddenly became inconspicuous.

The arrival was a tall man, well dressed, his lug-
gage expensive and heavy. His features were very
remarkable; they were features, once seen, never
to be forgotten. He seemed fairly young, virile and
energetic. When he removed his straw hat to wipe
the dust from his face, he displayed a high, narrow
brow that was white with the pallor of the city.

Beneath this brow were straight black eyebrows
like a bar across his face. The eyes, too, were
black—an intense and glittering black, luminous as
black crystal. A finely trimmed black vandyke
shaded his mouth, but accentuated the high, thin
lines of his countenance. The whole face was undeniably aristocratic, very handsome in a mesmeric
way, yet it held an indefinable hint of vulpine. The
stranger's hands were long, white, powerful.

"I have a friend, a Mr. Lee," said the stranger
to Piute Tomkins. His voice was smooth and very
self-assured, pregnant with authority. "He has, I
believe, engaged a room in advance of my coming?"

"He ain't," returned Piute, surveying the stranger. "But come in and eat, 'less ye want to miss
dinner. I guess we can rustle a room somehow.
We're havin' a treemenjous boom right now and all
the bellhops is off to the gold rush, but I s'pose we
can put ye up."

The spectators grinned at this elaborate irony.
The stranger, however, fastened his black eyes upon
Piute, and after a few seconds Piute began to look
uncomfortable.

"Ah, you are a very facetious gentleman!" said
the stranger coolly. "May I inquire if Mr. Lee
is stopping here?"

"Yep," said Piute, reddening a trifle. "He's
up in his room with a busted leg—but ye'd better

pile in to dinner 'fore seein' him. Dinner don't last long here."

"I hope not," said the stranger, going toward the hotel doorway, while the crowd guffawed at the confusion of Piute Tomkins.

Bill Hobbs, with incredulity in his eyes, slid into the hotel office and, listened unashamedly while the stranger conversed with Piute. The conversation was largely concerned with Tom Lee, and Piute got some information which made his eyes widen. Willyum got the same information; and, when the stranger was gone from the office, he sidled up to the desk and inspected the register. He saw that the stranger had signed as "James Scudder, M.D." of San Francisco.

"Gee!" Bill Hobbs grinned suddenly. "He ain't even usin' a alleyas, huh? Gee! I got a real story to write up now——"

Forgetful of dinner, he turned and put for his office across the street in a burst of feverish energy. Once there, he seized a pencil and began to scribble down what he had overheard, and then grabbed a stick and turned to the nearest type-case. In another moment the butchery was going forward merrily.

In the meantime, Doctor Scudder finished a hasty meal and then was taken to the room of Tom Lee. Presently he was sitting beside the latter's bed and inquiring into the accident.

In the adjoining room sat Claire Lee, busy with some sewing; but there was a flutter of fear in her eyes, and from time to time her lips trembled, as though she were fighting down some inner repulsion, some frightful and unspeakable horror whose talons were gripping at her from that inner room. And yet the two men, whose conversation came clearly to her, were not speaking of her at all.

"You wired me that you had found the place—the

place which exactly suited you," said Scudder calmly. "So I came right along."

"Good!" said Tom Lee, who was sitting up in bed. "Good! I am eager to get to work. Did you arrange for a contractor as I ordered?"

The doctor nodded.

"Yes. I stopped in Meteorite and got hold of a good man there. He's coming over this afternoon —drives his own car—and you can go over the plans with him to-night. Of course, you'll have to figure on expensive work, for men and supplies will have to be shipped from Meteorite by truck."

Tom Lee waved his hand negligently, as though the question of expense were one to be waived altogether.

"That goes without saying," he responded. "But I am glad that you came; I need you very badly. The allowance of opium that you gave me ran out four days ago."

Scudder laughed, and relaxed in his chair.

"And how are you doing without it?" he inquired. "Can you get along?"

"Not here in bed," he rejoined. "If I were outside, actively engaged, at work upon our plans, I think that the activity would help me tremendously. When I was busy with Claire looking up the place, I found this to be true."

Scudder's black eyes narrowed very slightly, as though inwardly he were a bit astonished. But his words gave the lie to this supposition.

"That's exactly what I calculated on," he returned easily, "and it proves that my theories have been correct. Fortunately, I brought along a good supply. By the way, I'm interested in this fellow who fixed you up—did you say his name was Murray? What did he look like?"

Tom Lee described Murray very accurately. From Scudder broke a word of astonishment.

"By George!" he exclaimed. "Do you know, that's very remarkable!"

"What?" demanded Tom Lee, gazing at him with heavy-lidded calm.

"That he should turn up here!" Scudder was animated, vigorous.

"You know him, then?"

"No, but I know of him. Why, that fellow was one of the greatest surgeons in the country until a year ago! He went all to pieces in a hurry and dropped out of sight; it was more or less hushed up, of course, but in professional circles the truth is known. It was caused by morphia; the poor fellow must have been a hopeless victim."

"He does not look it now," said Tom Lee. His features contracted slightly. "Morphia! And that goes back to opium again. All the more need of our getting to work without further delay, Doctor Scudder! You will remain here for a time?"

Scudder's eyes went for an instant to the door of the other room.

"Yes, as long as you want me," he rejoined. "In fact, I think I'll remain here until things shape up right, then return to San Francisco for my things, and come back here for good. I'll want to keep an eye on the building work."

Silently, without a word, Tom Lee took from a table beside the bed a little round cup of horn. Once it had contained a brownish substance, but now it was scraped clean inside, scraped down to the very horn. Silently, he held it out to the doctor. It was an opium *toy*.

Scudder smiled and nodded as he took the little cup. "I'll attend to it at once," he said, and rose. "Do you like this desert country as much as you expected?"

"Yes," said Tom Lee gravely. "It is wonderful;

it is ideal! I like it for itself, no less than for our
purpose. I am an American; I love this country, I
am part of it—and this desert is to me like the great
wilderness of my own Shensi, the very heart of the
ancient land, full of great unguessed things and
strange powers! Yes, I like this desert."

Scudder, shrugging his shoulders as though to
indicate that it was all a matter of choice, turned
away. At the door of the other room, Claire halted
him.

"Doctor! Is it true—what you said about Doctor Murray?"

For a moment Scudder looked into her eyes as
though reading what lay behind her eagerness, her
compassionate words. Beneath his beard, his lips
tightened.

"Yes," he said. "I'm sorry to say that's quite
true, Miss Lee. Of course, this Murray may not be
the same man. I'm delighted by your father's im-
provement; I think this country is going to do won-
ders for him! If you'll excuse me, I'll get him a
little opium now. It'll help him greatly and put him
in shape to go over things with the contractor to-
night."

He left for his own room, which was across the
hall. When the door had closed behind him, Claire
Lee stood motionless, both hands at her breast. In
her eyes was a numbed, wondering look, the look of
one who was inwardly fluttering with fear of the
unknown and the intangible. Then, as Tom Lee
called her, the look vanished and she turned to the
other room.

Tom Lee looked up at her, then held out his hand.
She took it, silently, and his strong fingers closed upon hers in a mutely significant gesture. It was an
endearment, that quiet touching of the hands, but it
was more than an endearment. From the massive
personality of the man there went out to the girl

a quiet force, a compellant for poise; a reassurance
of strength and faith and love unassailable.

"You are not glad he has come?" asked Tom Lee,
watching her eyes.

"No," she answered simply. "I do not believe in
him!" A wistful smile came to her lips, as she
touched his coarse black hair with caressing fingers.

"My dear," said Tom Lee gravely, "he has done
great things for me; his treatment is helping me tremendously. He is efficient, that man!"

Claire said no more. She turned away and opened
a box that lay upon the table. From it she took a
lamp, filled the bowl with peanut oil—which is odor-
less—and lighted it. She laid out a bamboo opium
pipe, a needle, a set of the simple, but ingenious
scales, and then turned again as Doctor Scudder
knocked and entered the room.

Late that afternoon, two other men drifted into
Two Palms. One came from the north, and this
was Deadoak Stevens. He tramped disconsolately
into the hotel and sought out Piute Tomkins, with
whom he was closeted for some time. The two men
emerged from their talk with an air of hopelessness;
Piute had chewed at his ragged mustache until it
had become a wisp.

The other arrival was the Meteorite contractor,
by name Patrick Hennesy. He greeted Piute jovi-
ally; a brawny, red-faced man, and registered for
the night. Then he inquired for Doctor Scudder,
and was directed to the latter's room. As he
turned from the register, he was frowning.

"What's this?" he said, beckoning to Piute and
pointing with one stubby finger to the register.
"Who's this guy Mackintavers? He don't go by
the front name o' Sandy, I suppose?"

Piute assented with a trace of surprise. Patrick
Hennesy broke into a lurid oath and inquired as to
the whereabouts of said Mackintavers. When in-

formed that Sandy was then somewhere to northward, he doubled up one huge fist.

"What's bitin' you?" inquired Piute with interest.
"Know him, do you?"

"Know him?" Hennesy glared for a minute, then
relaxed. "Well, I used to know him—and I sure
want to see if he comes back to-night! If he don't
—then don't say nothin' about me, savvy? I'll con-
nect with that cuss later."

Piute assented, not knowing just what to make
of all this. He felt too hopeless over the report of
Deadoak Stevens, however, to push his inquiries
into the matter.

Bill Hobbs, in the interim, was working feverishly
through the hot afternoon in his printing office
across the street. He had already evolved some
principles of type setting, and now he was alternate-
ly cursing and blessing the implements to his hand,
as he set up a grotesque and fearful array of words.

Toward sunset he viewed his labors with a mar-
velling satisfaction. The late proprietor had left
a front-page form already in shape to receive news
articles, and Bill Hobbs hung over the stone with an
admiring eye as he studied the news article which he
had supplied in part.

"Gee!" Willyum sucked in his breath admiringly.
"I'll break off for supper, then do some more. To-
morrow I'll have her done. Gee! Ain't she great!"

That evening he continued his labors by lamp-
light.

In the room of Tom Lee across in the hotel, Patrick Hennesy was that evening poring over blue
prints and architect's plans, discussing them with
Tom Lee and Doctor Scudder, while Claire listened
and made occasional comments. Hennesy looked
completely stumped and extremely mystified. He
was unable to arrive at the purpose of the buildings
which Tom Lee wished him to erect, and the prob-

able cost of them staggered him. But when Tom Lee calmly extended him a check which ran into four large figures, and told him to take it on account, he was forced to accept matters.

"Then I'll be back later," he said in conclusion. "I'll run out to that place soon's you got the deed, and see just what gradin' will have to be done, and git a shovel to work."

Early in the morning, the contractor departed back to Meteorite, repulsing all efforts of Piute and Deadoak to penetrate his mysterious business with Tom Lee.

Through the morning, Bill Hobbs slaved in his printing office. At noon, he announced jubilantly to Piute and other citizens of Two Palms, over the dinner table, that his forms were locked and on the press, and that he'd run off a newspaper that afternoon that would sure make 'em sit up some when they read it!

At two o'clock, after some slight delays incidental to inking and other complicated matters, the *Heln-gon Star* went to press.

"Gee!" exclaimed Willyum as he drew the first sheet away and looked it over with humble devotion in his eyes. "Gee! Ain't that wonderful, now?"

He was right. It *was* wonderful.

CHAPTER IX

THE NEWS STORY

THE last game of cribbage had been settled, and Haywire Smithers had departed to his own place; Mrs. Tomkins had come home from the weekly meeting of the Two Palms Ladies' Aid and had gone up to bed; and Piute Tomkins was locking

up for the night when Murray and Sandy Mackintavers came in from Morongo Valley—dusty, sun-
bitten, and hungry.

Piute listened sadly to their request for grub, and
agreed to rustle up some. He was no longer proud
and haughty before them; he had given up the un-
equal battle and had ceased to struggle. Virtue had
descended gloomily upon him, even as a mantle.

"Step into the dinin' room, gents, and I'll discover
somethin'," he announced.

"How's my patient?" asked Murray, pausing en
route to the wash room.

"The chink? All right. Say, I reckon ye ain't
heard the news about him?" Piute went back to his
desk and procured a sheet of paper. "And about
Scudder, too. Your friend sure busted somethin'
in these parts, he sure did! Look over this here
paper; it come out to-day, and I guess Scudder ain't
seen it yet. I want to be watchin' when he does see
it, that's all! Then I got a business proposal to lay
before ye whilst ye eat."

Murray took the sheet, and an ejaculation
broke from him as he saw that it was the first issue
of Willyum's paper. He hurried after Sandy, made
haste to get the sand and alkali out of his eyes and
hair, and passed into the dining room. Piute lighted
a lamp, and the two friends settled down to peruse
the astounding results of Bill Hobbs's labors.

Mere print cannot reproduce the phenomenon.
Mere printers cannot set in type all that Willyum,
in his blissful ignorance, had achieved in that pri-
mary issue of the revived *Helngon Star*. The date
had been unchanged. The advertisements along
the sides had been untouched; yet Willyum had
managed to fill four columns, by dint of ornaments
and other aids to progress.

The news story touched first upon Tom Lee, and
was begun with this lead:

We got in our   midst todaⲄ tmo guys thaꞀ come direct from
tHe hall oJ & Fame iNtwo tHe sentrel Presinct oF Two Palms₷
tHe misterY has beeu sollved:*

The article went on to say, more or less legibly,
that Tom Lee was immensely wealthy, and that he
owned a string of oriental shops in the Bay region
of San Francisco. He was, in fact, a magnate pure
and simple in the antique line, and was rated many
times a millionaire.

"Aiblins, now," observed Sandy, puzzling over
the page with knotted brows, "Bill is tryin' to say
somethin' about a man named Scudder, but I ain't
right sure———"

Piute joined them, bringing in some dishes. "Scudder is a doc," he put in, "and a friend of the Chinee.
I'd say, offhand, that he's due to raise partic'lar hell
about to-morrow, when he sees that there paper!"

Murray whistled, as he perused the paper. "Say,
Sandy—listen here!"

Willyum's remarks on Doctor Scudder were
frankly illuminating about Willyum himself:

I wunst seen tHis gInk iN neworLeens.?; wHen i was vagGed
ɐnd hE was iN tHe dOck two for pedLing dopǝ & Happy dust
two the nIgge*rs & jUdje give hIm hEll,? for it———

Willyum's remarks, apparently, knew no shame
over the fact that he had been "vagged"; but they
excoriated Doctor Scudder as a peddler of "dream-
books" and a supplier of dope.

They went on to say that Scudder had been forced
to leave New Orleans for his own health; that he
had there been a "dope" supplier to the underworld.
In language of beautiful simplicity, Willyum said
that Doctor Scudder was a top-notch crook and
would murder his grandmother for a dollar.

Sandy broke into a roar of laughter, but Murray
frowned gravely.

"Willyum's asleep now, I imagine—well, let him rest in peace until to-morrow! He's in bad."

"How come?" queried Mackintavers, while Piute stood by the kitchen door and listened hard.

"Libel. If these things aren't true, this man Scudder can just about rake the hair off Willyum! Confound it all, you go and put your foot in it when I'm not around, and then Bill Hobbs goes and does the same thing! Why, Scudder can sue for big dam-ages———"

"Huh!" grunted Sandy complacently. "Let him sue! You can't draw blood out of a turnip, not even with the law to help ye. So this Tom Lee is a rich man, is he? That's interestin'."

Murray nodded. "Seems to be. Queer what he's doing here, Sandy! But the girl—the girl Claire! I tell you, she's white! That's the queerest thing of all."

Piute came forward, bearing coffee and flapjacks, and sat down to light his corncob. He wore a por-tentous and solemn air.

"Ye don't think there's nothin' wrong, do ye?" he asked.

"No," said Murray decisively. "Nothing. It's something we don't understand, but it's nothing wrong. Tom Lee is no ordinary man."

"I reckon not," said Piute drily. "He done of-fered five thousand for Morongo Valley."

The two friends quickly glanced at each other, then stared at Piute.

"Five thousand?" repeated Sandy, incredulous.

"Yep. Now I'm putting it straight up to you gents, layin' all cards down, and leavin' it to you to do the right thing if ye sell to him. He wants to see you and buy the property. I guess you'll sell at *that* figger, huh?"

Murray leaned back in his chair and gazed at Sandy.

"It's up to you, Mac," he said briefly.

"What's he want?" "the minin' rights or———?"

"The whole works," returned Piute. "Or so he allowed. ·All of it!"

"No tellin' his game," quoth Sandy. "Doc, find out his object when ye see him in the mornin', and we'll talk it over."

Murray nodded assent, astonished and mystified by such an offer for Morongo Valley. He was too weary to discuss it now, however, and he wended his way to bed without further delay.

Early in the morning he was aroused by voices, and sat up. Sandy, who occupied a second bed in the same room, was talking with Bill Hobbs, and the latter turned to Murray with a proud but modest grin.

"Hello, Doc! Mac says you seen the paper last night. Kinda nifty, ain't it?"

"A miracle," said Murray gravely. "How you did it, I can't figure out yet!"

"Oh, printin' ain't so much," observed Bill loftily. "There was a few mistakes, I seen on read-in' her over, but next time she'll come through bet-ter. But what's this Mac is tellin' me about gettin' in bad?"

"All depends," responded Murray. "That story about Doctor Scudder—where on earth did you get the nerve to print that, you big boob?"

"Why, it's true!" asserted Willyum stoutly. "I was vagged down to N'Orleans, just like I printed it, and seen him in court bein' tried for supplyin' dust an' hop to———"

"Was he convicted?" demanded Murray.

"Nope. He slid through; his pals squared the bulls, I guess."

"Good Lord!" Murray began to dress. "Well, he can't get any money out of you, that's some satisfaction."

"Well, I ain't worried none," said Bill. "Leavin'

all that out, how did the paper strike you—honest,
now?"

"Great stuff, Willyum," responded Murray,
whereat the earnest William glowed delightedly.
"You've hit your vocation, if you can make it pay in
these parts. You get to work learnin' how to print,
and we'll look into the business end of it. If it
seems likely to pay, then we'll all put it through together."

"That's treatin' me white, Doc," answered Bill.

"Well," said Murray thoughtfully, "what we'll
do, I don't know yet." He turned to Sandy and put
the issue squarely up to him.

"I'll see Tom Lee after breakfast. If there's no
valid reason for keeping the place, why not make a
good profit while we can? Let him take the whole
place—unless you think there is any reason to keep
it."

The mining man stared reflectively out of the win-
dow.

"There is and there ain't," he said slowly. "I'll
be frank with ye, Murray— that place out there at-
tracts me! We could settle there and make a fair
livin' from the valley itself, what with the water
there and all. Aiblins, now the quartz will pay, too.
It's not big, but I'm thinking it runs big later on.
Lookin' at it from the development angle, instead o'
from the prospector's viewpoint, it might be worth
keeping."

"All right, then we'll keep it." Murray turned
to the doorway. "Come on down and let's get
breakfast."

Half an hour later, the three partners were just
pushing back their chairs from the breakfast table
when they caught the sound of loud voices coming
from the hotel office. The voices drew nearer, then
in the doorway appeared the figures of Doctor Scudder and Piute.

"That's him," and Piute pointed out Bill Hobbs.

His face white with anger, a copy of the *Helngon Star* clenched in his hand, Doctor Scudder faced the amateur printer with blazing indignation.

"This is an outrage! As sure as my name is Scudder, I'll have you jailed for this criminal——"

Murray stepped between the two men, in an attempt to pacify his brother physician.

"One moment, sir," he intervened. "Our friend here is not a printer and has allowed himself to be carried too far through his unfortunate ignorance of the libel laws. As a professional man myself I can realize how you must feel; but if you will allow me to explain the matter——"

Murray checked himself. In the blazing black eyes of Scudder he suddenly read a scornful anger that was now directed against himself.

"I don't desire any explanation from a man of your character, Doctor Murray," snapped Scudder. "I recognize you; you are the once eminent member of a profession which you disgraced! I have exposed you to Mr. Lee and his daughter in your true colors, as a dope fiend and one who should have been long ago ejected from the medical fraternity——"

It was at this point that the fist of Murray collided violently with the countenance of his colleague. Doctor Scudder was flung backward, caught his foot against a chair, and fell into the corner; he sat there motionless, staring up with one hand clapped against his bruised cheek, in his eyes an expression of dazed, but virulent enmity.

"That'll be enough from you," said Murray, standing over him. "If you want to argue the matter any further, get up! You don't want to, eh? All right. I'd advise you to go mighty slow with your libel talk against Mr. Hobbs, because if you start anything, I fancy that I would have a pretty good case of malicious slander against you. So think it over."

Murray turned away and left the dining room with his friends. Outside, he quickly hushed their indignant utterances; he was once more cool and calm, entirely master of himself again.

"Let the matter drop right here," he said briefly. "That fellow won't make any more trouble; our best bet is to leave him absolutely alone. I'll go up now and see Tom Lee."

He ascended the stairway to the upstairs hall, and knocked at the entrance of the two rooms occupied by the Lees.

Claire admitted him. Beneath her radiant greeting he noticed as he had previously noticed, the undefinable shadow that hovered in her eyes. The shadow, he thought, had deepened since he had last seen her.

Tom Lee was awake and expecting him. Murray returned the greeting of the big Chinaman, then met the latter's inflexible gaze with a square challenge.

"I understand," he said quietly, "that your friend Doctor Scudder is here. I presume, naturally, that you would prefer to have him in charge of the case. He has just advised me that he has made you aware of certain facts——"

Tom Lee lifted his hand commandingly.

"I am very sorry," he said, "that you and Doctor Scudder have had any misunderstanding, as your manner would imply. He told us a little of your story, not in any unkindly spirit, but simply because the mention of your name drew the memory from him. I wish you to retain charge of the case by all means. When you have looked at my leg, please sit down; I want to speak with you."

Murray bowed. He examined the injured knee, pronounced it to be mending in good shape, and in-

formed the patient that in another two days he
could walk a little. At a gesture from Tom Lee, he
took the chair beside the bed. The oriental gazed
at him for a moment, then spoke. "I know from my
own experience that you are a man of great skill.
I understand from Doctor Scudder that you were
at one time a victim of morphia, but I can see very
plainly that you have overcome this danger."

In the manner of the speaker there was a serene
calm that quite swept aside any possible search after
information. Tom Lee continued, his gaze holding
that of Murray.

"We may speak frankly, Doctor Murray. For
many years I was a victim of opium. I was born in
this country, and in business affairs I have become a
rich and even powerful man; but I have never succeeded in getting loose from the chains of the poppy.
Some time ago, I came in contact with Doctor Scudder, a man who has had great experience with drug
users. He undertook to cure me, and I believe that
he is succeeding."

Murray listened to this confession in some astonishment. The oriental did not speak with any symp-
tom of shame. He seemed to face the matter in a
very blunt and straightfordward way, which was very
significant of the man's strong character.

"I determined," pursued Tom Lee, "to devote
a portion of my wealth to helping others of my race
to rid themselves of the opium habit. To this end
I have been seeking a place which will be out of the
world and remote from any accessibility to the drug.
This portion of the desert, with its climate and situation, is ideal for my purpose. I propose to erect
a sanitarium and colony at my own cost, and to main-
tain it myself.

"Since meeting you, I believe that you can assist
me. Doctor Scudder, who has agreed to give my
enterprise the benefit of his knowledge and skill, is

a thoroughly good physician. I shall also need a
surgeon, however, and I believe that you can fill
that position admirably if you will. After much
search, the spot which I have chosen is the place
called Morongo Valley, north of here. I understand that you have recently bought it. I will be
glad to buy it back from you at any price you may
consider; and will make a flat offer of five thousand
dollars."

Murray listened to this proposal in astounded silence. He realized that this man was one who swept
aside all small things, and who dealt upon a large
and broad scale with everything and everyone.

Thus he was not so much surprised at the offer to
use his services, as at the outline of Tom Lee's business in this part of the country and the philanthropic
ambitions of the Chinaman. Before the man, he
felt ashamed. When he contrasted his own endeavors, and those of Mackintavers, to scheme and
obtain Morongo Valley and keep it, with the frankly
stated aims of this yellow man, he felt very small.
He felt dwarfed before the personality of Tom
Lee.

"My two friends have joined me in buying this
land," he answered slowly. He did not do his patient the injustice of considering the offered position
in the light of a bribe to sell the valley. "If we sell
to you at this figure, we shall make a profit—yet we
had already decided not to sell it. Mr. Mackintavers thinks there is gold in those hills——"

Tom Lee smiled. "Keep the gold, then," he
said. "Listen! I have my plans all drawn, ready
for work. I have in prospect a hundred more of my
countrymen—most of them my own employees—in
San Francisco, who have consented to break with
opium if I will help them. My idea is to keep them
at physical work—to use them here in the construc-
tion of my buildings, and in reclaiming the soil—as

a part of the cure. If you and your friends wish to work a mine, I will provide the labor. Why not? Keep the mining rights to the land if you wish."

Murray's face cleared. "That is eminently fair," he said reflectively. From the outer room had come a murmur of voices, and as Claire now appeared he rose. "I'll speak with my partners about it, and let you know. As concerns your offer of a position —may I reserve judgment upon that for a time?"

"There is no hurry," said Tom Lee, and looked at Claire.

"Doctor Scudder was here but would not come in," said the girl, a faint color in her cheeks. Murray, catching her glance, read a strange expression in her eyes, an expression so fleeting and indefinable that it wakened him instantly to the sense of something unusual. What had Scudder said out there? What did the girl think of Tom Lee's proposals?

"You have heard our conversation, Miss Lee," said Murray quickly, turning to her with his swift disarming smile. "May I inquire whether you think me a fit person to be associated in such a work?"

She met his gaze squarely, although her color deepened a trifle.

"I should be only too glad," she answered him, "to know that you would accept!"

He was surprised by the evident sincerity of her words.

"Something queer about all this!" he thought to himself, when he had taken his departure and was on his way downstairs. "Something queer about Scudder, too—I shouldn't wonder if Willyum had told the truth about him! And Clairedelune seems afraid of something. A white girl, I could swear, and as good as she is beautiful. What is her origin, then? Where is the answer to this riddle?"

He passed across the street to the printing office, where he found Mackintavers awaiting him. He

told the two exactly what had been said, and they
held a long discussion. Bill Hobbs swore that there
was something crooked about anything with which
Doctor Scudder was connected; but Murray, more
correctly, considered that Bill was prejudiced.   In
the end, they decided to accept Tom Lee's offer.   As
soon as Willyum was established in his printing
office, Murray and Sandy Mackintavers were to
visit Morongo Valley on a more extended prospecting trip.

Their first business was to get Willyum settled.
Ascertaining from the subscription list of the late
proprietor that there was a goodly scattering of
ranchers and homesteaders and prospectors about
the district and learning that a newspaper would be
welcomed and supported by some advertising, all
three partners got down to steady work.

Sandy and Murray canvassed the town with no
little success.   Two days later, a derelict in human
shape blew in from the south, having heard that a
paper was to be started in Two Palms.   He was a
hobo printer, a shiftless fellow who would be worthless to any real establishment—but to Bill Hobbs
he was a providential shower of manna.   Bill engaged him on the spot as preceptor.

During the three days which elapsed thus, Murray saw Claire Lee at intervals. He also informed
Tom Lee of the decision regarding Morongo
Valley, received a check for five thousand dollars,
and made over the deed to the land in the name of
Claire, as requested.   He and his friends encountered Doctor Scudder frequently, but the encounters
were very cold and formal.

On the third evening Patrick Hennesy arrived
from Meteorite in his car, and was at once closeted
with Tom Lee.   As the latter was still confined to
his room by Murray's orders, supper was served
there by Piute.   Hennesy beckoned Piute aside.

"Is that fellow Mackintavers still here?" he demanded in a grim whisper.

Piute allowed that he was.

"Then don't say nothin', but fix it up for me to meet him back o' the hotel early in the morning—all alone. Will ye? I don't want no interference."

Piute grinned suddenly.

"Will I?" he retorted. "Say! Them fellers—I put 'em next to a sale for their prop'ty, all fair and square; and they didn't even so much as slide me a ten-spot! Ain't that gratitood? I'm askin' ye—ain't it? Well, don't you worry none, Hennesy!"

"Ain't you a deputy sheriff?" demanded the contractor.

"Me an' Deadoak is both depitties. Why?"

"Tell you later," and Patrick Hennesy winked joyfully at Piute.

CHAPTER X

FLIGHT

UPON the following morning, Murray was at the printing establishment watching Bill Hobbs and his human derelict swear at each other, when Piute Tomkins beckoned him outside to the street.

Piute stood there, ostentatiously fingered a burnished deputy's star which adorned his sun-faded vest, twirled his melancholy mustache and spoke.

"Doc, the pris'ner wants to see ye."

"Prisoner? What prisoner?"

"Your partner, Mac."

"Good lord!" Murray stared blankly at him. "You don't mean he's—arrested?"

"Certain."

"On what charge?"

"Assault with 'tent to kill. Him and another man been mixin' it up consid'able back of the hotel; other man's Hennesy, the contractor from Meteorite. Seems like Mac took after him with an ol' wagon spoke and nigh riled him to death. I got him locked up in an extry room, so come along."

Murray followed, bewildered and angered. Sandy arrested!

Piute led the way into the hotel, and to a room at the door of which stood Deadoak Stevens on guard. A stern and implacable proponent of justice, Deadoak was also possessed of a polished badge and an ancient revolver, both of which he displayed with ostentation.

"Hennesy's goin' right back to town," he informed Piute, "he wants to see ye 'fore he pulls out."

Piute strode away.

Murray, meantime, entered the room, where he found Mackintavers sitting, the picture of disconsolate despair. Sandy glanced up, then dropped a battered countenance into his hands and groaned.

"Hello!" said Murray cheerfully. "Hear you've been fighting. What's the fun about?"

"Doc, it's no use," groaned Sandy. "I'm a branded man! I thought nobody'd know me around here—but along comes a man named Hennesy, a man whom I'd had dealin's with in New Mexico. Fact is, I made him leave there for his health. Now he's turned up here. I run up against him—wham! Then we went to it, that's all."

"I hope," said Murray, "that you hurt him worse than he hurt you?"

"I done my best," was the gloomy response. "I sure knocked him out—then this here deputy sheriff dropped a gun on me."

Deadoak Stevens introduced his head inside the door, which he had placed ajar.

"He's goin' to Meteorite after the sheriff," he

announced, "and you'll stay right here until he gets back——"

"Nonsense!" declared Murray. I'll bail him out and——"

"There ain't no one here to bail him out to," said Deadoak. "You got to wait, that's all. Ding my dogs, this here ain't no city!"

"Don't you try to stick with me, Doc," said Mackintavers hopelessly. "It ain't fair to you an' Hobbs. Things like this'll come croppin' up all the while ——"

"Don't be a fool," snapped Murray, and rose. "I'll see what can be done, Sandy. We'll take care of this fellow somehow. Did you have a wagonspoke in your hand?"

"I don't know," said Sandy. "I was hittin' him with everything in sight."

Murray chuckled and left the room.

He saw Piute Tomkins in the office downstairs, and speedily found that there was no way of freeing Mackintavers until the sheriff arrived in person. Piute flatly refused to accept bail, and there was no justice of the peace in town—the one and only J. P. being at the moment some score of miles away looking for a tungsten mine in the Saddleback hills. Murray gave up the attempt in disgust.

As he left the office, he saw that an automobile was standing at one side of the hotel, its engine purring. Standing talking to the driver was Doctor Scudder. Scudder stepped back, waved his hand, and the car drove away in the direction of Meteorite. Too late to halt the driver, Murray realized that it must be the man with whom Sandy had mixed. But what business had the man with Doctor Scudder?

Scudder passed him with a single flashing look, and Murray went on across the street, where he imparted to Bill Hobbs what had happened. They were still debating the matter, when the doorway was darkened—and Murray looked up to see Claire Lee.

She had already met Bill Hobbs, and had displayed much interest in his activities. But now she responded to Willyum's greeting with only a faint smile, and turned to Murray a gaze that was distinctly troubled.

"Doctor Murray," she said, a trace of color in her cheeks, "will you take me up to Morongo Valley in your car—right away?"

Murray was taken aback by this flat request.

"I—why, Miss Lee, what do you mean? Your father can't travel yet——"

"It's not a question of my father," she said, biting her lip. "Here is a note that he asked me to hand you——"

She extended a paper, which the astounded Murray took and opened. The note was brief:

My dear Doctor Murray:
     Please do as Claire says—and don't delay or ask questions.

TOM LEE.

Murray looked from Bill Hobbs to Claire, and choked down the questions that rose to his lips.

"When do you want to go?"

"Now," said the girl quietly. "I'll get my things in a few minutes."

" How long do you want to stay?"

"Until we hear from my father."

"Hadn't I better see him——?"

"No. He wants me to go at once."

Murray scratched his red thatch, more embarrassed and put to confusion than he cared to admit. This thing was preposterous on its face! No reason assigned—nothing but the request to take this girl away out there to the Morongo Valley, for an indefinite stay!

He looked helplessly at Bill Hobbs. "Willyum, can you take care of Sandy?"

"Sure," asserted Willyum, wide-eyed.

"I am at your service, Miss Lee," said Murray.

"You—you are very good, Doctor," she said, and he thought that her lip trembled. "I'll be ready in five minutes."

"Very well. I'll meet you behind the hotel, at my car—it's the one stacked with supplies in the back seat."

She turned and left the print shop. Bill Hobbs looked at Murray bewilderedly.

"What's it mean, Doc?"

"How the devil do I know?" Murray swore in puzzled disgust.

"Looked to me like she'd been cryin', Doc."

Murray swore again, and started for the door.

"Come on and help me throw some things together—put one of those extra gas cans in the back of my car, will you? Fortunately she's full up on everything. And you'll have to get Sandy's money before the sheriff gets it——"

They crossed to the hotel, and while he prepared for the trip, Murray instructed his henchman, whom he placed in charge of the mutual funds, to explain matters to Sandy and to do whatever might be possible.

The two men descended to the car, which was already filled with a mass of supplies made ready by Murray and Sandy against their return to the valley on a prolonged prospecting trip. Willyum turned over the engine, and as he did so, Claire appeared, bearing only a small handbag.

The anxiety in her countenance broke in a smiling greeting, and she climbed in beside Murray. The latter shoved down on his pedal and sent the flivver toward the street. He waved a hasty farewell to Bill Hobbs; and as he did so, a backward glance showed him the tall figure of Doctor Scudder, standing in the doorway of the hotel and gazing after them. Somehow, the remembrance of that impassive, high-browed, jet-bearded figure left a feeling of disquiet within him.

Not until they had left Two Palms behind them, was the silence broken. Then Murray, seeing Claire's handkerchief going to her eyes, put on the brakes.

"What's the matter?" he exclaimed.

"Nothing—please go on!" The girl forced a smile. "I'll tell you what's happened—I'll tell you what's happened——"

Murray drove on frowning. Presently Claire spoke, her voice low.

"You'll have to try and understand everything, Doctor Murray; I know that you're a gentleman, and father agrees with me. He isn't an ordinary Chinaman, you know—a coolie. Before the revolution, he went into business. He consolidated a number of antique shops near San Francisco into one big combine, and he's wealthy. But he has so set his heart on doing good to other men who have the opium habit, and helping them to break it, that whoever can approach him in the right way can— can win his trust. Doctor Scudder has done this."

"Ah!" said Murray. "You don't like Scudder, eh?"

"I don't trust him!" exclaimed the girl passionately. "I think he's been deliberately keeping Father under the influence of opium, while pretending to cure him; a doctor can obtain the drug now, you know, and no one else can. Well, this morning I met Doctor Scudder in the hall, and he said something—something I resented, and when I told

Father, there was a row. I'll have to be perfectly frank about it, Doctor Murray.

"Doctor Scudder apologized to me and said I had misunderstood him, then he launched a bitter attack on you and said that he meant to prove you were not what you seemed to be at all—that you were engaged in smuggling drugs——"

"I?" exclaimed Murray, then laughed amusedly. "Nonsense!"

"Well, there was a fuss," said the girl. "I hoped that Father might begin to see Doctor Scudder as I saw him; but I don't know—it's terribly hard to tell just what he thinks and does not think, for he seldom says anything. When we were alone, he told me to take that note out to you, and to have you take me to Morongo Valley at once—without any delay."

"And no reason given?" asked Murray, in open astonishment.

"None," she responded. "I thought that perhaps he wanted to get you away from Doctor Scudder, to prevent trouble; but why should I go too? He refused absolutely to explain anything."

Murray reflected that there might be excellent reasons for the girl going too, but that certainly none appeared.

"Well," he said whimsically, "since we're on our way, we might as well go! I certainly am honored and delighted by your company, Miss Lee. I think you're a very wonderful sort of woman, and that your father should send you with me, like this, implies a trust which I shall try to deserve.'"

The girl glanced at him, and to his amazement he saw that a smile was rippling in her face.

"You've been wondering about me, I suppose? Most people do; they seem to think that it must be terrible to acknowledge a Chinaman as one's father, and to love him! I remember that when some of

the girls came home with me one vacation, they
could not see the wealth and happiness around me,
the devoted servants such as they had never been
used to, the love and affection which had been flung
about me.   All they could see was the yellow man
who was their host——"

Her voice trailed off, and suddenly Murray realized that her smile had not been one of mirth.   A
quick flash of pity leaped through him.   He saw
her life as it must be—always a stigma upon her,
always the yellow man whom she loved and who
loved her, always the shadow that enveloped her
friendships and all that she did!

"A year ago, Miss Lee," he said quietly, "I was
among the leaders of my profession.   Through the
deadly sin of heedlessness, of failure to observe what
I was doing in the effort always to do more in my
profession, I became a drug fiend.   Since then, I
have conquered myself—but in the world's eyes I
can never be rehabilitated.   So I, too, have learned
the folly of caring what the world thinks or says.
It is the inward self that matters; nothing else."

"Oh, but you are cynical about it!" she answered
simply.   "Rather, you are trying to be cynical, and
not succeeding very well.   Haven't you found that
after all life is very good as it is—that in one sense
the world does not matter, but that in another sense
one must regard it very keenly?   To be thought ill
of, hurts, and hurts much.   There is always self-
respect, and the inner guidance of one's own life to
be followed; but all the same, one must bring one's
self into accord with the things outside.

"It does not worry me to be considered the
daughter of a yellow man.   I am only sorry that
people cannot know, as I know, the wonderful character and goodness of Tom Lee.   Why, if he is able
to do what he came here to do, he will be a tremendous benefactor of his own race!   Hundreds

of the men who work for him are still slaves to opium, although most of them would be glad to be free again."

Murray followed the road mechanically. It was a poor road, merely a track across the white-gray desert face, dodging to avoid ancient "Joshua trees" or groups of cacti, ever following the line of least resistance and curving endlessly.

The road did not interest Murray; he was thinking of the girl beside him and her situation.

"At least," he said gravely, "I think that I can appreciate the character of your father; and if I were you, I wouldn't worry about my own position. You're a marvelously beautiful girl, Clairedelune—beautiful beyond words, and with a deep fund of personality to back it. To have your trust and confidence and affection would be an unbounded honor to any man alive! For you to think, perhaps, that any man who cared for you might be prejudiced because there is Chinese blood in your——"

"Oh!" cried out the girl suddenly. Her voice startled him, shook him. He saw that her face had mantled with crimson. "Oh! But that isn't so!"

"What?" Murray turned toward her, slowed the car, stared uneasily at her. She met his gaze with level eyes, although her bosom was heaving tumultuously.

"I thought you knew!" she exclaimed. "I'm only an adopted daughter, Doctor Murray; father found me in San Francisco at the time of the fire, and could never discover my real parents. So he adopted me——".

"Adopted you? Would such a thing be allowed?"

"Yes, for all the records were destroyed; besides, at that time Father was known as a Manchu prince, and his position was highly respected. To save trouble, Father merely took the adoption for granted; it was never legal, perhaps, but it was never questioned. And so——"

Murray sat in a daze, unable to find words in the astounded comprehension that burst upon him. He could see only the one great fact—that she was bred of no oriental race! He knew now that he must have been prejudiced before that supposition; he had fought the prejudice, had conquered it, but none the less he felt a surge of relief, and a song uprose in his heart.

Then he told himself that he was a fool to think such thoughts. What matter to him? As to what the girl had suggested about his being a drug smuggler, quoting Scudder, Murray never gave this another thought. He forgot it completely.

CHAPTER XI

THE SUN STRIKES

MORE than once did Murray curse himself for a fool as he piloted the car northward into the wastes, but he continued his course without delay.

The girl's story had moved him strangely, stirred him to the depths. Still it was not clear to him why he was thus taking Claire out into the desert—except that he was compelled thereto by the dominant will and massive personality of Tom Lee. To tell the truth, Murray was far from urging upon himself any logical reasoning for what he was doing; the presence of Claire beside him was reason enough. He was joyful at the intimacy established between them, at the friendly confidence that had risen. It was long since Douglas Murray had craved the company of a woman—and now he felt strangely happy and buoyant.

They were in the marble cañon now, and repairing a tire that had blown out. There was about them the full heat of a desert day, sickening and insufferable. The white walls of the cañon, where was no shade or relief from the blinding dazzle of the white sun, refracted the heat tenfold and shimmered before their eyes in waves of smoldering fire. All breeze was dead. The car, where the sunlight smote it, was blistering to the touch.

Murray got the tire repaired, and with a deep sigh of relief flung the jack into the car. He refilled the boiled-over radiator from one of the water canteens swinging beside the car, then climbed under the wheel. He paused to mop his streaming face.

"Do you think your father means to come out to Morongo Valley?"

"I think so, with the contractor—perhaps tomorrow or today. Really, Doctor Murray, I can't say just what he intends! When Father gives no explanation of his actions he simply is inscrutable."

Murray nodded and started the car forward. He could well understand that Tom Lee, masked by oriental calm and being governed by the unfathomable oriental mind, was, even to Claire, an absolutely unknown quantity.

They cleared the cañon at last. Here was not the table-flat desert, however. From the canyon the trail debouched into a wilderness of volcanic ash and wind-eroded pinnacles, where along the rocky portals great smears of smoke-weed hung wavering like the wraith of long-dead fires.

From here, at last, back to the desert—and into one of those salt sinks of the desert, a basin of some ancient sea, perhaps, where the road wound precariously between stretches of sun-baked, salty earth that none the less quivered to the touch of any object, and formed at the bottom of the baked crust a quagmire from which was no escape. The fiery air made the travelers gasp as each parched gust of breath smote their lungs; and the salty, invisible dust stung their skins and choked their throats with remorseless burning.

And in this cockpit of hell, the blistering heat combined with the rarefied atmosphere to blow out another tire—and to blow it out this time beyond repair.

"Whew!" exclaimed Murray disconsolately, viewing the damage. "Nothing for it but to strip her and put on the other spare."

"Can't you run on the rim?" queried Claire anxiously.

"No chance, with this load of stuff in back, and the road we must follow! We'd smash every spring in the car. Well, here goes!"

There was no breeze. The far vistas of the horizon hung dancing with heat waves, like painted scenery jerking on springs. Mountains and mirages, all hung there and danced, a weird dance of death and desolation.

The unstirred air was heavy and thick with invisible dust. Sunlight crawled and slavered white-hot brilliance over everything, pierced into everything. His face running with blinding sweat, Murray impatiently threw aside his hat. Presently his unruly red hair was no longer wet and blackened; it crowned his flushed features like an aureole, crisp and dry and very hot.

He had the new tube and casing on, and attached the pump. Laboring steadily, he cursed to himself at the heat—the broiling, insufferably dry heat of that salt basin. A sudden breath of hot air caused him to glance up, and his lips cracked in a smile. Claire was leaning from the car and fanning him, her straw hat flapping the air down over him.

"Thanks, Clairedelune," he croaked hoarsely. "It helps."

"Will you have a drink? The water bottle——"

"No, thanks. I'll finish this job first."

The tire was beginning to harden. He bent again over the pump, driving himself to the labor. At last it was done—done well enough, at least. He disconnected the pump and tossed it into the car. A word from Claire broke in upon him.

"What's that! Something moved against the sand—oh! It's a snake!"

He laughed unsteadily as he looked. A snake in truth—an incoherent, feeble object that slipped across the sand and blended there, shapeless and indistinct; a stark-blind thing, a living volute of death and venom. Murray flung a handful of sand. The reptile lashed out viciously at the air.

"A rattler shedding its old skin; blind and deadly poisonous at this season," he said. "I remember Mackintavers warned us about it—no rattles, no sound at all!" He laughed, for his own voice astonished him; it sounded thin and tenuous, far away, distant.

With a distinct effort of the will, he forced himself to stoop after the jack; disengaging it, he rose and lifted it into the tonneau, with strange effort. Claire got out of the car in order to let him in more easily, but he did not climb into the shadow of the top. Instead, he held to the open door for an instant, then sank down upon the running board.

"I think I'll rest," he said, looking from bloodshot eyes at the figure of the girl beside him—the slender, cool figure that seemed to defy the sunlight. "Clairedelune—it comes from the troubadours, that name—the softly sweet glory of the silven moonlight—the sheer beauty that wrings the heart and soul of a man with pain and sweetness——"

His head jerked suddenly. As though some inner instinct had wakened to fear and danger within him, his voice broke out sharply, clearly:

"No cold water, mind! It kills—no cold water, mind!"

Not until his head fell back into the car doorway did Claire Lee realize that something was actually wrong. She had thought him babbling a bit—now, for a terrible moment, she thought him dead.

Yet his last words abode with her, remained fixed and distinct in her mind. No cold water! His heart was beating; he was not dead after all. He must have realized, in that moment, what the trouble was! Sunstroke. She realized it now, realized it with a fearful sense of her own futility. She had no water, except the ice-cold water in the porous waterbags beside the car!

Hesitation and fear, but only for an instant. She seized the nearest bag, her hands trembling in desperate haste, and jerked out the cork. Part of that precious fluid she poured into the sands, then stumbled to the front of the car and stooped to the pet-cock of the blistering radiator. As the hot water poured into the bag, she could feel its coldness change to a tepid warmth. Hastily she ran back to Murray and poured the contents of the bag over his head and shoulders.

She grew calmer, now; he was at least alive, and she had done her best! But there was more to do. Morongo Valley lay ahead, not so far, and she knew the road. With much effort, she lifted the unconscious body into the front seat, where it reposed limply, and then climbed over it. She had forgotten to crank the car, and had to go back again, out into the sunlight.

No word, no cry from her clenched lips. She cranked, climbed again into the car, and closed the door that would hold Murray in place. Then she drove, with an occasional frantic glance at the lurching, senseless man beside her.

She drove as fast as she dared set the car through

the loose sands. When she had driven that road first, it was trackless. Now there lay faint markings to guide her—the tracks of her own and of Murray's car, the shuffled traces of hooves and feet.

No wind ever lifted in this basin, no flurry of sand ever drove across the burning surface, down below the level of the surrounding desert. Until the rains or a storm came, the tracks would be there undisturbed, as the dust-marks within a pyramid of ancient Rameses.

Soon, so soon that she scarce realized it, the blue and brown mountains that had been trembling over the horizon were drawn into sharper and richer colorings, and the long walls of the valley were opening out ahead. The Dead Mountains, those—bare of men or beasts or devils!

Morongo Valley at last—the sharp turn, with the Box Cañon opening out ahead, rich and sweetly splendid in its touch of vivid greens!

It was only two hundred yards in length, after that turn; yet to the tortured girl, those two hundred yards seemed endless. She did not pause at the shack, but drove on, toward the right-hand wall. Still within her mind dwelt the last words uttered by Murray—"no cold water!"

The trickle of the creek was icy cold; out of the ground and in again. But she knew where there was a seepage of warmer water—water unfit for drinking. She had found it while she was here with Tom Lee; it was a little up the hillside, above and facing that natural amphitheatre which Tom Lee had staked out as a building site. About it there was shade, for the water had provoked green growths on the hillside—a clump of green there against the brown.

She knew that this was the spot, and she headed for it. Recklessly, she drove the car at the steep hill, rocking and lurching across gullies and rocks,

until the engine died down; then in low again, climb-
ing a mad course, until at last a boulder blocked the
wheel and the engine died on the crash.

There was but a little way to go. She got Murray out of the car, somehow, and dragged him,
spurred by fear that she had been too late in getting here. Yet he still lived.

She laid him on his back in the course of the tiny
seepage of water—and then it seemed so cold to
her that new fear gripped on her soul. She tasted
it, and grimaced. It was not cold, and it was brack-
ish, impregnated with minerals. So slight was the
flow, that it existed for little more than the length
of Murray's body. And there was not the shade
here that she had anticipated—it was too slight,
too little, here at noonday!

That was easily remedied. A trip to the car, and
she had opened Murray's lashed bundles. A trip
down the hillside to the shack provided her with
stakes. From four of these she stretched a blanket
above the recumbent man, and saw that now the
congestion had died out of his face. He was breathing more easily, too.

Then reaction came upon her, and bodily weari-
ness, and flooding tears.

She rallied, however, and fell to work. By mid-
afternoon she had accomplished much. Seeing no
hope of moving Murray to the shack, she made another low canopy of blankets, preparatory to remov-
ing him from the seepage; opened out provisions,
brought up a tiny sheet-iron stove from the shack—
it would be cold with the night, bitter cold! There
were many things to be done, and her hands were un-
accustomed to doing these things; but she did them.
And when they were done, she took the hand-ax she
found in the car, and sallied down past the shack in
search of firewood, for the hillside was bare.

When she returned, and came into sight of the

camp, she dropped her burden and ran forward; for
Murray was standing there in the sunlight, one hand
to his head, staring around him dazedly!

Her cry of protest swung him about. He managed a wan smile, then obeyed her imperative,
panted orders and dropped beneath the blanket
canopy she had erected. She came up to him,
breathless with effort and fear.

"The sun got me, eh?" murmured Murray.
"Clairedelune, you're a wonder! I don't see how
you did it. Lord but I feel ill again———"

He dropped back limply, and she burst into tears
of despair and helplessness as she knelt above him.

Again she lashed herself to work, removed the
blanket from above the seepage, and laid it aside
for a night-covering. A Californian, she knew little about sunstroke; but she believed that now he
had fallen into a coma, which might pass into sleep,
and his regular breathing gave her some assurance.

The afternoon dragged into evening, and the
night came. Still Murray lay senseless, breathing
heavily but evenly. The sun slipped out of sight
under the western rim, and darkness clamped down
until the stars shone.

Claire spread her blankets above the tiny shelter
she had made for Murray, and lay with her face
to the south and Two Palms. What time it was
when she wakened, she did not know; she lay for
a moment wondering why she had roused, then
glanced toward Murray's shelter. In the starlight
she could see that he had not moved. She could
hear his breathing, as it had been. Then—her
gaze leaped to the desert floor, where two moving
stars were drawing close.

An automobile! Hope sprang within her, drew
a quick, glad cry from her lips. She leaped up and
arranged her dress with shaking fingers. Tom Lee
was coming, then, was almost here!

Hurriedly she made shift to light a tiny blaze from the fragments of her fire, to guide the arrivals. As the car came into the valley below, the sound apprised her that it was a flivver, and she became certain that Tom Lee had come. The car threaded its way up the hillside, and ten feet from Murray's car, came to a halt. Its engine was not shut off, and its headlights held Claire in the center of this scene, lighting the place dimly, but efficiently.

Two dark figures leaped from the car and came toward her. A cry broke from Claire, and she drew back—not Tom Lee after all! Here was Piute Tomkins, and with him a stranger whom she did not know. But her fear vanished swiftly, and she choked down her disappointment.

"I'm *so* glad you came!" she exclaimed. "Doctor Murray has been hurt—why, what's the matter?"

She halted, blankly astounded. The stranger and Piute both produced revolvers, and their manner was distinctly unfriendly. The stranger now flashed the badge of a sheriff; he was a keen-eyed man, bronzed and resolute.

"You're under arrest, Miss Lee," he said. "So is Doctor Murray. That him yonder?"

"Arrest?" faltered the girl, shrinking in amazement and fear.

"Yep, complicity," said Piute. "The doc had a lot of opium in his room, and morphine—and you're helpin' him in his getaway! This here is the sheriff—Hennesy sent him over a-flyin'——"

"But—but it's impossible!" wailed the girl, anguish in her voice. "He's ill—he's had sunstroke! And he's never had any opium——"

The sheriff, who seemed to dislike his job, shook his head. "Sorry, Miss Lee, but we got the goods on him. My car broke down and we had to impress Bill Hobbs to bring us out here——"

At this instant another figure came into the rays of light from the car. It was Bill Hobbs.

"What's the matter, Miss Lee?" he demanded. "Where's the doc?"

"He's ill—he had to fix a tire and the sun made him ill," she said weakly. "These men are trying to arrest him and me—oh, it's ridiculous!"

"Gee!" breathed Willyum, staring from her to the recumbent figure beneath the blankets. Then he swung on the other two. "So that was why you had me run you out here, huh? Tryin' to make a pinch, huh? You kept darned quiet about it!"

"Enough for you," snapped the sheriff. "Get busy, and help carry that man——"

Suddenly Bill Hobbs changed. In a moment, he became a new man. Across his face swept an altered look; his hand leaped to his armpit, and an automatic flickered out toward the two men. He took them completely by surprise, covered them before their weapons could lift.

"Put up yer mitts!" he breathed hoarsely, a wild light in his flaring eyes. "Put 'em up, youse! So help me, if I gotta croak you——"

The two obeyed, utterly astounded.

"You'll do time for this," began the sheriff furiously. Bill Hobbs flung an excited, reckless laugh at him.

"Will I? You'll go to hell first! Now look here—the doc ain't done nothin' at all, and you'd ought to know it! You big stool, you," Bill cast the words venomously at Piute. "I'll cook ye for this!"

"Hey! It wasn't me!" spoke up Piute in obvious alarm. "It was Doc Scudder! Don't go to p'inting that there gun too reckless——"

"Scudder, was it?" Bill Hobbs swore. "I said that gink was crooked! So he tried to frame the doc, here, did he?"

"Good lord!" uttered the sheriff suddenly. He

had been staring hard at Bill Hobbs; now he took a step backward, across his face flitting a look of recognition. "It's Swifty Bill!"

Willyum snarled at him.

"Yah, Swifty Bill!" he jeered. "Seen me before, have ye?"

"I've got pictures of you, my man," said the sheriff. "And word that you're wanted in Memphis—you've been wanted there for a long time! Those handbills have been up on my office wall for three years—why I didn't know you before, I can't say why——"

Bill Hobbs spat a vicious oath at him. Claire had shrunk back, white-faced and fearful, watching the intense scene before her with eyes that only half comprehended.

"Know me, do you?" flung out Bill Hobbs. "And ye'll try to pinch one o' Swifty Bill's mob, will ye? I guess not! The doc ain't done nothin', I tell you! Youse guys ain't goin' to frame him an' get away with it, not for a minute!"

"See here," broke out the sheriff. "You're trying to buck the Government, Swifty Bill, and you know what *that* means! This man Murray had a lot of opium and morphine in his possession, and has no permit for it. You'd better put down that gun——"

"I got that gat down on *you*," said Bill firmly, "and she stays like she is."

Suddenly he paused, then broke out anew, an impulsive eagerness brightening in his face.

"Say! What d'you guys say to this—leave the girl an' the doc go, and take me with you? I'll go! How's that, now? If ye want me, all right. If ye don't, I'll sure croak both of youse if we don't blow out o' here!"

Piute looked at the sheriff, but the latter scarcely hesitated. Those three-year-old handbills on the

wall of his office recurred to his memory; Swifty
Bill was implicated in a federal job back in Memphis, and there was more credit to be gained from
the capture of such a man, than from taking in
Murray.   Besides, the drugs had been confiscated,
and the chances were that Murray could not be pun-
ished for merely having them in his possession.

"You're on!" said the sheriff quickly.

"Then leave your guns and beat it to the car.
I'll come in a minute."

The sheriff nodded to Piute.   The two men dropped their weapons and retraced their steps.   After
watching them for an instant, Bill Hobbs turned to
Claire Lee, and gestured toward Murray; his eyes
were suddenly brimming with devoted affection.

"He ain't dead, miss?"

"No—but he's very ill——"

"Listen!   I gotta beat it with these guys, see?
When we get to Two Palms, I'll wise up your dad.
I guess the doc ain't bad hurt.   What's in this dope
frame-up, anyhow?"

"I don't know—it's all some mistake," said Claire
vaguely.

"All right, then.   Say, tell the doc I'm squarin'
things up, will you?   Him and me's pals, see.   Tell
him, will you?"

Claire nodded dumbly.   So quickly had the situation evolved itself, that she was not yet fully
sensible of its significance.   The meaning of all this
rapid-fire exchange of words was as yet only partially
comprehensible to her.   She could only nod assent.

Bill Hobbs turned and stumbled away to the car
and the waiting handcuffs.

CHAPTER XII

SCUDDER COMES

THE night passed, and the day, and another
night, dragging their weary length above Morongo Valley.   After the car that bore Piute, Willyum, and the sheriff had vanished over the desert
horizon, that horizon had remained unbroken.   No
one had come.

Murray slept the clock around, and wakened
hungry but very weak.   All strength seemed to
have fled out of him.   The rare sunstroke of the
desert had smitten fiercely.   When he heard Claire's
narrative of what had happened during the preced-
ing night, his first thought was to get back to the aid
of Bill Hobbs; but when the girl inspected the car,
she pronounced the task hopeless.

"The front axle's all crooked, and the left wheel
is half twisted off," she reported, her eyes resting
upon him anxiously.   "I must have done it getting
up here——"

"No matter," said Murray, losing all energy.
The least movement appeared to drain his strength.
The slightest touch of that blinding sunlight sent his
brain whirling and reeling.

"I give up," he went on.   "I'm good for nothing.
Take a look around for rattlers; you have to watch
out for them this season, for they give no warning
but strike blindly—and they're bad medicine.   Lord,
but I'm helpless!"

As he lay there, he reviewed the girl's story of the
attempted arrest, and believed that he understood it
very plainly, although he did not attempt to explain
matters to Claire.   She had enough to worry her,
he decided.

He remembered that Scudder had been talking

with the contractor when Hennesy left to get the sheriff. He knew already that Scudder had opium, for the use of Tom Lee. It would have been no hard matter for Scudder to have planted some of the drug among his own effects, he reflected.

"I'll settle with you, Scudder!" he vowed to himself.

Toward sunset they searched the horizon, but vainly. What was happening beyond that horizon, over the rim of the world? Murray worried, more about his friends than himself, for he was little concerned over Scudder's enmity and attempts to disprove him in the eyes of Tom Lee.

But Sandy Mackintavers was in the toils, and as for Bill Hobbs—Murray groaned at the thought. He knew that Willyum had only recently come out of "stir" when he had picked up the ex-burglar. Now that Bill Hobbs had deliberately sacrificed himself in order to save Murray and Claire Lee, it meant a setback that would put him in the criminal ranks again for good. And at this moment, when both his friends needed him so sorely, Murray was stretched out here in the desert, helpless and impotent—himself under the menace of a cloud!

During that day, Murray and the girl lived long, came to know each other deeply; not with the superficial words and phrases and acts of civilized life, but in primitive ways and fashions. When the night closed down again like a mantle above the desert, it drew them yet closer together.

"Your father will be here tomorrow at latest," said Murray reflectively.

"He should have come long ago." Claire's eyes were filled with somber shadows. "I'm afraid that —that Doctor Scudder has been keeping him under the influence of opium. How I detest and fear that man! I wish that Father could be made to see him as I see him, that he would break with the man!"

"I think he will, eventually," said Murray, and smiled grimly to himself at thought of the reckoning he would have with Scudder.

The night passed. Once, Murray wakened; it seemed to him that he caught, in the desert silence and cold stillness, the throbbing motor of an automobile. Yet he could see no lights, and Claire had not wakened. He lay for a space, watching vainly, and at last fell asleep again.

With the morning, Murray opened his eyes to find Claire already up and breakfast nearly ready. He tried to rise, and managed to leave his blankets, but he was giddy and too weak to walk. With a muttered curse at his own feebleness, he sank down again upon the sand.

"If no one shows up here by afternoon," he declared resolutely, while they breakfasted and discussed the situation, "I think we'd better make an effort to get back with the car. She may run; when it comes to flivvers, the days of miracles are by no means over——"

At this instant, Claire sprang to her feet with a cry of joy.

"Look—look! A car!"

Murray twisted around, and saw a moving object upon the desert face. From where they were upon the hillside, it was possible to see only the stretch of the cañon floor immediately below them; a twist in the cañon walls hid the remainder of the road from their sight, until it came out again upon the desert basin half a mile away. It was out there, crawling in from the low horizon, that the moving automobile appeared.

"It's Father!" cried the girl, watching the car intently as it rapidly drew closer to them. "It's our car! I know it because we had to put the license plate on the right fender—oh, I'm so glad. Now everything's all right!"

Silence fell upon them both. They watched without further speech as the car came in toward them, and finally vanished from sight. Five minutes later, it appeared down below in the little valley, its cheerful thrum reverberating upon the morning silence, echoing back from the cañon walls. But, as Claire watched, uneasiness grew in her eyes.

There was but one man in the car, the driver. The flivver was halted down by the shack, and its driver alighted. Murray glanced at the girl, and read a swift flutter of fear in her eyes.

"It's not Father at all—it's Doctor Scudder!" she breathed.

"Don't worry," said Murray coolly. "I expect your father sent him here. Ah, he's coming up! That's good."

His calm manner exerted a quieting effect upon Claire. Toward them from the cañon climbed Doctor Scudder. As he came closer, his cheery "Good morning!" floated to them, and both Murray and Claire made answer. Scudder completed the climb, panting a little, and removed his hat to wipe his brow.

"Where's Father?" exclaimed Claire eagerly.

"I'm sorry to say, Miss Lee, that he's not well," returned Scudder, his eyes taking in each detail of the scene. "Hobbs came into town yesterday in custody of the sheriff, and told us of the situation here. Your father hoped to be able to come himself, but early this morning he was taken rather ill. So I came in his place."

"Did you give him more opium?" cried the girl accusingly. Scudder's brows lifted.

"No, I mean that he was really ill, Miss Lee. For the past two days he has not touched the drug, and his system is not yet inured to the deprivation. What's this, Murray—sunstroke? I hope you'll let me do anything in my power——'

"Thanks," said Murray quietly. Instinct told him that the words of Scudder were a tissue of lies, yet he knew that he was in need of the man's skill. "I'd like to have a talk with you all alone. Miss Lee, would you have any objection to leaving me and Doctor Scudder in private for a few moments?"

"Ah!" said Scudder suavely. "I was about to make the same request!" He smiled thinly. "And I have a very good excuse, Miss Lee. The contractor arrived yesterday to come out here with your father; but as their trip has been temporarily delayed, your father asked if you would take some pictures of the ground just back and above the place he had selected as a building site. It has something to do, I believe, with the building of a tank or a reservoir for water from the spring. You'll find the camera in the rear of the car."

"Very well," said Claire, with a nod of her head.

She departed down the hillside, and Scudder gazed reflectively after her, watching her lift the camera from his car, and then start toward the wall of manzanita that cloaked the upper end of the valley. Murray's voice caused him to turn.

"Well, Scudder, we'd better have a showdown," said Murray calmly, gazing up at the man. "The sheriff was out here, as you know, and told about finding dope in my belongings. What made you plant the dope there? That was a silly way to try and discredit me in the eyes of Tom Lee."

Scudder looked down at him and smiled. There was nothing mirthful in the smile, however. It was a cold, hard, deadly smile, like the fixed and drawn-back lips of a snake waiting to strike.

"You guessed right, Murray," he said unexpectedly. "It *was* a rather futile thing, and I've found a much better way. I don't mind telling you that I gave Tom Lee enough opium last night to keep him doped for a week, so there'll be no interference."

Murray swore. "You damned whelp!" he said, trying to raise himself, but vainly. "If——"

Scudder leaned forward and shoved him back in his place, with a chuckle.

"No more fisticuffs, eh?" he sneered. "Not in condition just now, are you? Well, I'll have you fixed up in no time! Morphia victim, weren't you? Well, I'll pump morphia into you for about three weeks—and turn you loose. That'll take care of you, I guess."

From his pocket, Scudder took a hypodermic case, and a bottle of tablets. He filled the tiny thimble-cup with water from the spring, dropped a tablet into it, unfolded the inch-square metal stand, and set the cup in place. Then he put the stand down, struck a match, and held it beneath the cup.

"Handy affair, this!" he observed.

Murray watched him in horror which changed from incredulity to realization that the man intended his words literally. Knowing that Murray had been a morphia victim, he was now deliberately taking advantage of his helplessness to inject the drug again—and with Murray in his charge, he could put him hopelessly under the spell of the drug once more!

"Good God, man!" cried Murray, getting up on one elbow. "You can't mean——"

Scudder put out a foot and shoved him back again.

"Lie put, will you?" he chuckled. "Wait till I get this syringe filled, and by the time Claire comes back, you'll be past speech! And you won't speak to her again until I'm ready to let you."

While he spoke, Scudder filled the syringe, and adjusted a needle. Then, the syringe in his hand, he came and stood over Murray.

"Struggling won't do you any good," he said, and bent down.

Murray struck at him—struck weakly and vainly. Scudder seized his right wrist and drew it down—put it under his foot and held it there. Then he seized Murray's left arm, gripped the wrist, and drew it up to meet the syringe.

"Now for happyland!" he said. "One slight prick——"

He paused suddenly—paused and jerked himself upright, a flood of color sweeping into his pale features as his head came up. From the clumps of manzanita twenty feet away, had come a voice.

"Hold on, Scudder!"

And from that covert of twisting, grotesque, blood-red manzanita trees, stepped Tom Lee. Murray felt something of the fright that had seized upon Scudder, for the presence of Tom Lee seemed nothing short of an apparition.

"I waited for this, Scudder!" rang out the voice of the yellow man, his eyes fastened upon the horrified gaze of Scudder. "When you gave me all that dope last night, I guessed that you were coming here; I discovered that you had planted the stuff in Doctor Murray's suitcase, I had begun to penetrate your wiles and deviltry! Now it's ended."

Tom Lee came forward. Before him, Scudder shrank. The syringe dropped from his nerveless fingers; he stepped back from the figure of Murray, retreated from the advancing form of Tom Lee in visible terror and consternation.

"You devil!" cried the oriental, a deep and surging passion filling his voice. "I came here last night in Hennesy's car—I've been waiting for you! I heard all your lies, heard all your plotted deviltry. You thought you'd dispose of Murray and have Claire in your power, didn't you?"

There was reason for the sheer terror that filled

Scudder. The face of the advancing man had changed into a frightful mask; it had changed and altered into the face of the great stone Buddha that watches over the Yungmen caves—it had become a purely Asian face, filled with terrible and deadly things, unguessed menaces.

Murray painfully got to one elbow again and watched. The others were oblivious of him; all their attention was fastened upon each other. Still Scudder retreated, and still Tom Lee advanced upon him, weaponless, yet in his advance a potent and fearful threat. Before that threat, Scudder still retreated, his face ghastly.

"Damn you!" he cried, his voice shrill. "What d'ye mean by all this——?"

"You can't get away from me," said Tom Lee impassively. "I'm going to have a reckoning with you."

"No, but I can stop your game!" retorted Scudder with an oath. The mask was gone now, and he cursed luridly. "You can't run any damned Chinese bluff on me——"

With the words, he plucked a revolver from his pocket and fired.

The shot echoed and reëchoed in the cañon. Tom Lee did not move. Scudder glared up at him and made as if to lift the weapon again, then he hurled it from him with another curse, and kicked at something on the sand at his feet. A shrill scream broke from him. Something fell away from his kick— an incoherent, feeble object that slipped to the sand and blended there, shapeless and invisible; a stark-blind thing, a living volute of death and venom—a rattler, that had struck blind, but that had struck home!

With that scream still on his lips, Scudder whirled about and began to run. He fled, as though after him pursued some invisible and awful thing. He

ran blindly down the valley as though in search of
something, desperate in his extremity; he passed
the automobile in which he had come, running, stum-
bling through the soft sand. And so out of sight
around the twist in the cañon.

"Let him go! It is finished."

The words came from Tom Lee. He turned to
Murray, smiling, and the smile seemed fastened in
his face. He lifted his arm, and looked at the hand,
curiously. A cry broke from Murray, for the hand
was streaming with a scarlet fluid.

Abruptly, Tom Lee pitched forward and lay in
a heap, just as Claire, called by the shot, appeared.

CHAPTER XIII

UNTANGLED

A FLIVVER that bore two men, came crawling
down the slope of the desert-rim in the early
morning. Near the approach to Morongo Valley,
it halted. The two men alighted to inspect a heap
in the sand, from which a carrion bird flapped heavily away. They looked at the body, glanced at
each other, then silently got into the car and continued their journey.

"Rattler, I judge," observed Sandy Mackintavers.
"And a good job."

The car crept up the valley to the shack, stopped,
coughed, and became silent. Murray was awaiting it, pale and weak but walking; beside him was
Claire, and joining them was Tom Lee, his right arm
in a sling.

Murray's face lighted up, and his hand shot out.

"Willyum!" he cried delightedly. "We thought
we must be dreaming when we saw you! And

Sandy too—but I thought you were behind the bars!"

Across the earnest features of Bill Hobbs broke a rippling light of gleeful mirth.

·"Say!" he exclaimed, while he pumped Murray's hand. "Say, I gotta hand it to that sheriff for bein' a prize boob! I was wanted all right—three years ago! Since then, I done the time an' got out again, see? When the answer come to his wire, that was the sickest guy you ever seen! But say, Doc, how are you?"

"Fine! Coming around all right." Murray's gaze went to Sandy Mackintavers. "What stroke of luck turned you loose, Sandy?"

The voice of Tom Lee interposed, with a chuckle.

"That was my doing, gentlemen," he said blandly. "The contractor, Hennesy, preferred to withdraw all charges against Mr. Mackintavers, to losing my contract. And, Mr. Mackintavers! I wish you'd come up the hill here. There's something I want to show you."

Sandy nodded and joined him, and the two men ascended toward the seepage where Murray had lain.

Bill Hobbs looked from the face of the girl, alight with a strange happiness, to the incisive, quizzical eyes of Murray. He seemed to sense a constraint, flushed slightly, and was turning away when Murray's hand halted him.

"Hold on there, Willyum! I'm glad, old man, very glad, that everything's clear for you! By the way, I've an item of news for your paper. You know what I told you about the sanitarium? Well, Mr. Lee is going ahead with his plans, and I'm to be in charge——"

"Say!" broke out Hobbs with sudden remembrance. "What happened to Scudder? We seen him out yonder, and Mac laid it to a rattler."

"Mac was right, I suppose," said Murray, thoughtfully. "Although I'm not so sure that it wasn't the hand of Providence, Willyum. But lay it to the rattler and play safe. He shot Tom Lee through the arm before the rattler got him; he sure had panic, blind panic! And, by the way, I have another item of news for you———"

Murray glanced at Claire, who smiled happily. "Miss Lee," he pursued, "has decided to chance being the wife of a country doctor."

A shout from the hillside drew their attention. Tom Lee was standing beside Claire's camp, and out of the seepage of water near by, shouting and waving his hands, was Sandy—dirty, streaked with sand and water, adrip with perspiration and exultancy.

"Aiblins, now, will ye look at this!" He pointed to the seepage, a blaze of excitement lighting his face.

"We see it," answered Murray, laughing. "What's the matter with it?"

"Matter with it?" shouted Sandy, waving his arm at the brow of the hill. "Free gold, that's what! It'll take us smack into rotten quartz, that's what!"

A little later, Bill Hobbs, standing by his automobile, rolled a cigarette.

"Aw!" he muttered to himself. "Aw, gee! And now I gotta go back to the printshop and work all alone with that old derelict—and Sandy's gotta work all alone at the mine—aw, gee! Ain't it hell how a woman busts up everything! I wisht I was a poor man again!"

www.ingramcontent.com/pod-product-compliance
Lightning Source LLC
Chambersburg PA
CBHW020147180626
46810CB00004B/1778